Mary Elizabeth Braddon

Flower and Weed

Mary Elizabeth Braddon

Flower and Weed

ISBN/EAN: 9783337041472

Printed in Europe, USA, Canada, Australia, Japan

Cover: Foto ©Andreas Hilbeck / pixelio.de

More available books at **www.hansebooks.com**

FLOWER AND WEED.

A NOVEL.

BY

M. E. BRADDON,

AUTHOR OF "LADY AUDLEY'S SECRET," ETC.

COPYRIGHT EDITION.

L E I P Z I G

BERNHARD TAUCHNITZ

1883.

The Right of Translation is reserved.

CONTENTS.

FLOWER AND WEED.

CHAPTER I.

A WAYSIDE WAIF.

"A lovely child she was, of looks serene,
    And motions which o'er things indifferent shed
    The grace and gentleness from whence they came."

INGLESHAW CASTLE is one of the historic homes
of England, built in the days of the Plantagenets,
improved and expanded in the reign of the last of
the Tudors, and never debased or deteriorated by
modern alterations, adaptations, or restorations. It
stands on low ground, in the heart of an extensive
chase, rich in deer and ground game—a wild woodland, where many of the great oaks and beeches
are as old as the establishment of the house of
Ingleshaw amongst the ruling families of England.
The Castle is built of dark-gray stone, rich in those
lovely gradations from deepest purple to palest green
which mark the long growth of lichens and mosses,

stealthily stealing over the stony surface, and touching it with beauty. There is a grand simplicity
about the noble Gothic entrance, and the great
square hall with its open roof; while there is all the
charm of quaintness and homeliness in the long low
passages, the deep-set windows, with here a bay
and there an oriel, to break the monotony of long
rows of heavily mullioned casements, giving an in-
sufficient light to the dusky old portraits and seven-
teenth-century pictures which line the panelled walls
of the low spacious rooms.

Ingleshaw is one of the show places of Kent,
but it is only shown when the family is away; and
on this bright May morning the family, beginning
and ending with Lord Ingleshaw and his only child,
Lady Lucille, is at home; and the tourist, thirsting
to steep himself in the historic associations of the
Castle, turns from the gate with reluctant feet. Perhaps there never was a more quiet household than
this of Ingleshaw Castle. There is something akin
to pain in the silence of the long corridors and the
empty suites of rooms, where the effigies of departed
Ingleshaws stare for ever at vacancy; where a bee
comes booming in at an open pane in the mullioned
window, hovers over a bowl of hothouse flowers on
a Florentine marble table, and goes booming out
again, disgusted at the dulness of life within stone

walls. Sometimes the ripple of girlish laughter floats
through an open window of the southern wing, or
the bird-like notes of a girlish soprano are heard
in the distance, singing one of Mozart's tenderest
melodies.

Lord Ingleshaw is something of a recluse, and
his only daughter has not yet made her entrance
upon the bustling theatre of society, to be elbowed
and hustled by that common herd to which the
doting father deems his child an infinitely superior
being. Her eighteenth birthday is terribly near,
and next year, the father tells himself, his innocent
simple-minded darling must needs be handed over
to the high priestesses of the temple of fashion;
must take her place in society, be wooed, won, and
wedded; and then it would be to him almost as if
he had no daughter. New associations, new loves,
new joys, new hopes, new cares, would arise for her
who was now all his own.

"Well, it is the common lot," he muses, dreaming in his library over an open folio of Bacon's
Essays or Sir Thomas Browne's *Urn Burial*. "I
must wait for a girl-grandchild, whom I may train
up to be something like the companion and friend
my little girl has been to me. She will last my
time. I shall be dead and gone before she need be
presented at Court."

He has a fixed idea that from the hour his daughter enters society she will be in great measure lost to him. This comes, perhaps, from his profound contempt for modern society, which he despises the more intensely because he has held himself aloof from the vortex, and only contemplates its foolishness from the outside. This external view of fashionable life is like a deaf man's view of a ball-room. Lord Ingleshaw sees the puppets dancing, without hearing the music which is their motive power; and the whole thing seems rank folly: folly treading on the heels of vice.

His sister, Lady Carlyon, a dowager countess, passing young for her years, as all dowager peeresses are nowadays, a lady who lives in society and for society, has told him that Lucille must take her proper place in the world, must be seen and admired and talked about, and even written about in the newspapers, before she can be properly and creditably married: and he is prepared to submit to the inevitable. He would rather his girl should be wooed by the interchange of a miniature and a few formal letters, and wedded by proxy, like a princess of the seventeenth century. Anything would be better than the turmoil and dissipation of fashionable society, the rubbing shoulders with doubtful beauty and tarnished rank, the inevitable brushing away of youth's tenderest bloom, sinless Eve's primitive innocence. One little year yet remains to the fond father. Lucille is not to be presented till next season. The Earl has begged hard for this extension of his happiness.

"She will be horridly old by that time," says Lady Carlyon, in her hard business-like way, staring at the unconscious Lucille, who is playing a dreamy gondollied of Mendelssohn's at the other end of the long low parlour. "I'm afraid she is one of those girls whose looks will go off early. Half the beauty of her eyes depends upon that cabbage-rose bloom of hers. Nothing tells so well as youthful freshness just now. It is the only attraction with which we can counter those horrid professional beauties. If Lucie's complexion goes off you can keep her at Ingleshaw all your life, for she'll make no great marriage."

"My heart's desire is to keep her here for ever," answers the Earl; "you talk of her as if she were a Circassian slave, waiting for the next market."

"That's stuff and nonsense," exclaimed Lady Carlyon; "I suppose you would like your daughter to make a good marriage?"

"I should like her to marry a good man."

"Well, we'll try to combine the two, though it isn't the easiest thing in the world."

This conversation took place in the Easter holidays, which Lady Carlyon spent with her brother and her niece, trying her hardest to inspire Lucille with a thirst for the amusements and delights of that privileged circle she was soon to enter, and making only a very faint impression upon the girl's mind. A cup which is already full can hold no more, and Lucie's life at Ingleshaw was completely happy. She adored her father—the father who had been all the world of kindred and affection to the motherless girl; she loved her good-natured old governess, Miss Marjorum, who had taught and trained her from her fifth year until now. She loved the historic old house, the romantic chase, the old gardens, lawns, and summer-houses, fish-pond, bowling-green, arbours, fountains—that happy blending of the Dutch and Italian style which gave such variety to the extensive grounds. She loved the grave gray old stable, the pretty little mouse-coloured Norwegian ponies which she drove, the senile white cob which she was permitted to ride unattended about the chase, and the handsome young bay mare which she rode on rare and happy occasions by her father's side. She had dogs, cats, and pets of all kinds. Most of the servants had seen her grow up, and all of them worshipped her. She lived in an atmosphere of love, and had never any sense of

dulness in the silent old house to which so few
visitors came.

Lord Ingleshaw was by no means a cipher in his
world, although he held himself aloof from fashionable society. He was a stanch Conservative and a
strong politician, voted upon all important measures,
spoke occasionally, and had weight and influence in
his party. He had a house in Grosvenor-square,
where he occupied three darksome rooms on the
ground-floor, leaving the upper and more splendid
apartments to gloom and disuse. The brief, bright,
happy period of his wedded life had been spent
partly in this house; and the rooms were haunted
by the sweet sad shadow of his young wife, who
died of a fever caught in Venice six months after
her baby's birth. For the greater part of the year
he lived at Ingleshaw, a bookworm and a recluse,
caring very little for any society except that of his
young daughter.

Father and child had breakfasted *tête-à-tête* this
bright May morning in a pretty little room called
the painted parlour—a gay cheery little room, with
panels painted with flowers and butterflies in a graceful fashion that savoured of the Pompadour period.
May was fast melting into June, and the windows
were wide open, and the room was filled with perfume from within and from without; flowers on tables,

chimneypiece, brackets, and a wilderness of flowers in the garden outside.

"What are you going to do with yourself this morning, pet?" asked the Earl, as his daughter hung over his chair. "Don't go and mew yourself up with Miss Marjorum in this delicious weather. All the other butterflies are enjoying their lives in the garden."

"I hope you don't think me quite so frivolous as the butterflies, father? Yes, it is a too delicious morning. I meant to read Dante with Miss Marjorum directly after breakfast; but I think I shall keep those poor things in the second circle waiting an hour or two while I have a ramble on Puck. Dear old Marjy won't mind."

She kissed her father, and was running off, when he stopped her.

"O, by the bye, Lucie, I forgot; I've some news for you. I had a telegram from Bruno last night."

"From Bruno!" she cried with clasped hands, while a lovely roseate hue crept over the alabaster fairness of face and throat; "and you never told me!"

"Well, I suppose I wanted to keep this bit of news for a pleasant surprise: only I never could keep a secret from my girl. The telegram is from Florence, and Bruno is coming home almost directly.

He will come straight here. You can tell Twyford to have his rooms got ready."

"Almost directly!" repeated Lucie. "What does that mean, father? To-day?"

"Hardly. He was in Florence yesterday."

"True, and Florence is at the other end of the world—a three days' journey at least. To think of his coming home so soon! His last letter was so vague."

"Will you be glad to have him at Ingelshaw?"

"Of course I shall be glad; but I shall see very little of him. He will be always rushing away somewhere—trout-fishing; or to London, or to Sevenoaks, or Tunbridge Wells. Thank goodness the hunting is all over. He can't be riding off at nine o'clock every morning to come home at half-past seven, all over mud."

"Make the most of him while you have him," said her father. "He is a man now, and will have to take his place in the world as the future Earl of Ingleshaw."

The girl dropped lightly on her father's knee, and nestled her head in his bosom.

"Don't!" she cried. "I can't bear you to talk of anybody coming after you. God grant that Bruno's head may be as white as snow before he is Earl of Ingleshaw."

"That would be to doom your father to long years of senility. However, Bruno is in no hurry, and I am in no hurry. He has a fair fortune, considerable talents, and I hope he will distinguish himself as Mr. Challoner before he is Lord Ingleshaw. And now run away and have your ramble. I shall be off to catch the express in half an hour, and I have to see Morley before I go."

Morley was his lordship's land-steward and factotum.

"Dear father, I am so sorry you must go to London. I hope you will be back before Sunday."

"Be sure I sha'n't stop in town longer than I am obliged; but I must wait to see this measure through the House."

"How I hate measures and the House, when they take you away from me!" said Lucille.

Now came tender farewell caresses; and then the girl raced off to the distant rooms which belonged to her and her governess. She had come to a delicious period of her life, in which the bondage of the schoolroom was done with, while the restraints of society had not yet begun. In her own small world, so safely hedged round by reverence and affection, she did very much as she liked, went where she liked, spent as much money as she liked, cultivated the people she liked. She was in some wise mistress of her father's house. She ruled the trusty old governess who had once ruled her; but though somewhat wilful as to those things upon which her impetuous young heart set itself, she was as docile and easily governed by a light hand as a thoroughbred horse.

"Marjy, Marjy!" she cried, bursting into the old schoolroom, now morning-room and study, where Miss Marjorum sat with dictionaries and grammars and Italian histories laid out before her, ready for tackling Dante,—"such news! Bruno is coming; Bruno will be here to-morrow, or, at furthest, the day after to-morrow!" 'And the bells shall be rung, and mass shall be sung,'" sang Lucie at the top of her clear young voice, "for my red-cross knight."

"This is indeed a surprise," said Miss Marjorum, without turning a hair. "Mr. Challoner coming to us after nearly two years' absence! I have no doubt he will be grown."

"Don't, Marjy; you mustn't say such things. It's actually insulting! Don't you know that Bruno is four-and-twenty?"

"Then he will have expanded," said Miss Marjorum. "It seems only yesterday that he came of age; and I know that up to that time he was continually growing in a perpendicular direction. After that he began to widen and spread horizontally, and he has been expanding ever since."

"Marjy dearest, you talk as if he were Falstaff, or bluff King Hal," cried the girl.

"My dear, all I wish to express is that he is a well-grown young man. And now, my love, let us attack our Dante. We are approaching one of the finest passages in the *Inferno*."

"Marjy dear, it is such a delicious morning, and this news about Bruno is so exciting, I think if I were to ramble in the chase for an hour or so, it would compose my mind and make me more equal to Dante."

"You must do as you like, my love; but I never find your intellect so much on the alert after those rambles in the chase. There is a marked tendency to yawning and inattention."

"You shall find me attentive to-day, dearest. But I must have one peep at the bluebells in Hazel Hollow. Think what a little while they last!"

"As you advance in life, Lady Lucille, you'll find that all earthly pleasures are as brief as the bloom of wild hyacinths," said Miss Marjorum, who fancied it a part of her duty to be for ever repeating trite moral lessons, and scraps of old-world wisdom.

Lucille skipped off to her dressing-room to put on the short-skirted shabby old habit in which she rode Puck; and then, light and swift of foot, ran down the broad oak staircase to a door that opened into the stable-yard, where a groom was waiting with Puck, a shaggy gray cob, of the Exmoor breed, hog maned, stoutly built, strong as a house, with an eye which beamed with kindness. Lucille generally mounted at this door, preferring to escape the ceremony of going forth under the great Gothic archway, where the prim matron who lived in the gateway turret looked out at her through the lattice of the parlour where the visitors' book was kept, or stood in the doorway to curtsy to her as she went by. The stable-yard opened into the park, and Lucille was away and out of sight of the Castle in five minutes.

It was one of those exquisite early summer mornings when to live and breathe the sweetness of the air is rapture; when the old feel young, and the young can scarce tread soberly upon the dull earth, moved to dance-measures by the ecstacy of mere existence. The soft warm flowery air crept round Lucille like a caress, as she rode slowly along a grassy ride, under the broad spreading boughs of a line of horse-chestnuts, the turf white with the fallen blossoms, and yet the trees bright

2*

with lingering bloom. Further on in the green
heart of the chase came a little wood of Spanish
chestnuts, leafy towers, their lowest boughs sweeping
the grass, their summits aspiring to the blue bright
sky. These grand old trees were planted wide
apart, and the intervening ground was a sheet of
azure bloom, save here and there where the drift
of last year's withered leaves showed a patch of
golden brown starred with wood anemones.

Beyond this chestnut plantation there stretched
an undulating expanse of open sward, with here a
beech and there an oak, standing up against the
summer sky in solitary grandeur, monarchs of the
woodland; and then came those wide oak and fir
plantations which bordered the chase for the breadth
of half a mile or so throughout the seven miles of
its circumference, rough and broken ground full of
gentle hollows and ridgy slopes, the paradise of
squirrels, rabbits, and wild flowers. Puck knew
every inch of those plantations, for he and his
mistress had roamed about in them at all hours
and in all weathers; sometimes when the snow lay
deep in the hollows, and the first of the wild snowdrops showed pale on the topmost ridges where the
sun had touched them.

Puck was accustomed to take his ease in these
woods, tethered to a tree, while Lucille wandered

on foot among the brown fir trunks, the gray lichen-clothed oaks, botanising, entomologising, sketching, or musing, as her fancy. prompted. Her childhood and girlhood had been passing lonely, save for Bruno Challoner's occasional companionship; and she had learnt to find her own amusements and her own occupations, more especially when the Earl was in London, or at Aix or Wiesbaden for his health, and life in the Castle meant a perpetual *tête-à-tête* with Miss Marjorum, who possessed every amiable quality except the power to amuse. In these woods Lucille had learned her lessons, day after day, from earliest spring to latest autumn; here she had read her favourite poets; here she had become familiar with all that is practical and interesting in the history of flowers and insects. The woods had been her playroom and study ever since she could re-member. To-day she let Puck crawl his slowest pace along the grassy rutty rides, stumbling a little now and then in a sleepy way, and recovering him-self with a jerk. She was thinking of that distant cousin of hers, Bruno Challoner, heir presumptive to yonder gray old castle, and the only friend and playfellow she had ever known, since the Vicar's four daughters, who were allowed to drink tea with her three or four times a year at the utmost, could hardly be called companions.

Bruno had spent a considerable portion of all his summer vacations at Ingleshaw. He had come here in the Long Vacation when he was an undergraduate of Christchurch; had read here—or made believe to read—with "coaches," classical and mathematical, soberly-clad gentlemen, in smoke-coloured spectacles, who had grown prematurely old in a perpetual grinding at Plato and Aristotle, or the integral and differential calculus; men who were steeped in stale tobacco, and who avoided Lucille as if she were a pestilence, so deep was their loathing of her sex. The classical coach was tall and thin, and wore his hair long. He had written poetry, and saw life on its Greek and ideal side. The mathematician was short, broad, and florid, and believed in nothing that could not be expressed by signs and figures.

Bruno went in enthusiastically for the Greek plays and the higher mathematics, but did not come out very strongly in either branch of learning. He got his degree, but it was by the skin of his teeth, as his tutor told him candidly. Since those Oxford days he had travelled a good deal for the improvement of his mind, at the instigation of Lord Ingleshaw, who was his guardian as well as his cousin; and now he was four-and-twenty, had been free of his kinsman's tutelage for the last three years, but was still beholden to him for counsel and friendship. He had made the tour of Europe, seen a little of Africa, and was coming home to begin the world as a man who, by the dignity of his future, and by all the traditions of his race, was constrained to make some figure on the stage of life.

"Dear old Bruno," thought Lucille, as she moved slowly, with sauntering rhythmical motion, under the flickering lights and shadows, amidst the spicy scent of the pines, "how glad I shall be to see him again! I wonder whether he will be as glad to see me?" She remembered their last parting, when she was not quite sixteen, and still had something of the awkwardness and shyness of early girlhood. She remembered the grave tenderness of his farewell, and how he had entreated her to think of him while he was far away; promising that in every day of his wandering life some loving thought of her, like a winged invisible messenger, should fly homeward to dear old Ingleshaw. Her desk was full of his letters from strange and ever-changing places, her rooms were beautified with his gifts. He had given her substantial reason to know that she had not been forgotten.

A feeble shy from the old pony—Puck, who seldom shied—startled the girl from her reverie. The drooping eyelids were lifted; and there, beside

the broad green track, lying in the hollow of a dry
shallow ditch, among mosses and bluebells, and the
last of the anemones, Lucille beheld the cause of
Puck's alarm.

A woman, quite a young woman—nay, a girl in
what should have been the first fresh bloom of girlhood—lay asleep in that mossy hollow, the azure
light of bluebells reflected on her wan pinched
cheek, one wasted hand lying pale and deathlike
among the flowers. The thin scanty cotton gown
hardly concealed the shrunken outline of the figure.
The feet, one bound in blood-stained rags, the other
in a boot which was the veriest apology for covering,
testified to long and weary tramping upon dusty
high-roads.

Lucille slipped from her saddle, and, with Puck's
bridle hanging on her arm, went close up to the
prostrate figure. It was not the first time she had
found a tramp asleep in Ingleshaw woods, nor the
first time that her immediate impulse had been to
relieve abject poverty, worthy or worthless, needing
no higher claim upon her charity than its piteous
condition. She stood looking down at the sleeper,
but more keenly interested than she had ever felt
before in any stray creature she had found in her
domain.

The face lying among the flowers was so beautiful, exquisitely beautiful, even in its pinched and haggard condition. The low broad brow, the delicate Greek nose, the heavily-moulded eyelids, with their dark thick lashes, the oval cheek from which the rich growth of bronze-brown hair was swept back in a tangled mass, the melancholy lines of the pale lips, the modelling of the small dimpled chin —all were perfect, and on all there was the stamp of sickness unto death. What could Lucille do? She had no purse with her, or perhaps she might have done no more than drop a sovereign into that shrunken hand, and pass upon her way. Yet there was something in the sleeper's face that would have haunted her painfully afterwards, had her charity gone no further than this. As it was, she tied Puck to a tree, and sat down at the root of another, within a yard or so of the sleeper, patiently to await her waking, in order to see what could be done with her.

She had not long to wait. Before she had been seated five minutes, looking dreamily at the sulphur-hued butterflies flitting across the mossy hollows where the wild hyacinths made broad patches of azure light, the flies grew too tormenting for Puck's patience. A sharp shake of his honest old gray head rattled bit and bridle, and at the sound that pale sleeper stirred uneasily, and the heavy lids were lifted from eyes darker than night.

Those dark velvety eyes looked up at Lucille, the pallid lips quivered faintly, and, as if with a painful effort, the wayfarer lifted herself into a sitting position.

"Lady," she murmured in a low hoarse voice; and then the tears gathered in the large dark eyes and rolled slowly down the haggard cheeks.

"Are you ill, or in pain?" asked Lucille gently.

"I have been ill, lady. I was laid up in the infirmary at the Union in London with a fever; and then I got well, and they turned me out; and I set out to walk to Dover, where I've a friend; but last night I was quite done, and I slept under a hay-stack a little way from here; and when I woke this morning I could hardly move, but I just crawled across a field, and in through a gap in the fence, and the place was cool and quiet, so I laid down to sleep, or to die—I didn't much care which. You wouldn't if you was me."

"You mustn't talk like that," said Lucille. "Are you hungry?"

"Not now, lady. I'm past that."

"And you are very tired?"

"Tired! Yes; all my bones ache with tired-ness."

"How old are you?"

"Somewheres between seventeen and eighteen. That's as much as I know."

"Have you no parents?"

"Never had none to remember."

"No relatives or friends?"

"None, except him that's at Dover."

"What is your name?"

"Bess."

"Your surname?"

"Never knowed. I was allus called Bess."

Lucille reflected for a minute or so, and then made up her mind what must be done with this worn-out wayfarer. It was more than a mile to the Castle, and it was evident that the girl could hardly walk half a dozen yards. She had dropped from sheer exhaustion. To offer her food and comfort and shelter at the end of a mile's walk would be as meaningless as to offer her a refuge in one of the stars without supplying the means of transit. No, there was only one thing to be done: Puck must carry this poor creature to the Castle.

"I want to take you to my father's house, and to give you food and rest," said Lucille. "Do you think you could sit upon my pony if I were to lead him? He's very quiet."

"I don't know, lady. I don't know as I could

stand on my feet. Things look all of a swim like, as if I was in a merry-go-round."

The weary head drooped upon Lady Lucille's shoulder as the girl spoke; the tangled dusty hair and gaudy cotton kerchief rested unrepulsed on the young lady's green habit. Never before had Lord Ingleshaw's daughter come into such close contact with squalid nameless poverty.

"We must get you on to the pony somehow," she said. "Rest your head against this tree while I bring him to you."

She left the girl leaning, limp and inert, against the red-brown fir-trunk, and went over to Puck, who was contentedly nibbling the soft flowery turf at his feet. Lucille led him to the spot where Bess reclined, and then lifted the languid form from the ground, Bess giving what help she could, but that of the feeblest. She was evidently in a half-fainting condition, and would have to be held on the pony.

The aged and slumberous Puck lent himself very placidly to the operation, though wondering at it. Lucille managed to lift the helpless girl on to the saddle, and to support her in a sitting position, drooping listlessly forward over Puck's mane, as she led the pony through the plantation, and by the nearest way to the Castle, crossing the broad stretch of velvet turf in the bright May sunshine.

All that glory of sunlight and greensward, old forest trees and fallow deer, the distant gleam of the lake in the hollow, the grandeur of the old Castle standing solid and gray against a wooded background, was lost on Bess, whose head was never raised from its drooping posture, and for whom this terrestrial globe was just now a dim dream hovering on the verge of darkness. It needed but the faintest swing of Life's pendulum to make all dark.

Lucille went into the stable-yard with her strange companion. It was dinner-time, and the men were away, all things in the yard still and slumberous as in the castle of the Sleeping Beauty; but at the sound of the pony's hoofs an old man came out of the stables, and advanced to meet his master's daughter.

This was Tom Pike, the old groom who had special charge of Puck. He had taught Lady Lucille to ride, before she was advanced enough for her father to take her in hand, and he worshipped her. So when she told him to take the tatterdemalion in his arms and carry her into the Castle, he had no power to gainsay her, albeit he felt the proceeding was altogether out of keeping.

One feeble protest, and one alone he made.

"Hadn't I better take her into the saddle-room, Lady Lucille? I can get her a bit of meat and drink there."

"Nonsense, Pike; the poor thing is dreadfully ill. She wants ever so much care and nursing. Just bring her where I show you."

Pike took Bess upon his shoulder, as if she had been a dead fawn, and carried her into the Castle, following Lucille, who led the way to a neat little bedchamber at the end of a long corridor, and very near to her own rooms. It was a room which was generally given to a visitor's maid, and had been lately occupied by Lady Carlyon's middle-aged abigail.

Here they laid the half-unconscious girl on the bed. As her head sank upon the pillow, her eyes closed, and she fell into a sleep which was almost stupor.

"Go down-stairs and get me a glass of port and a piece of sponge-cake, Pike. She must have something directly. She has been starved."

"Looks rather like it, Lady Lucille. But don't you think my lord will be angry with me for bringing such offal into the Castle? She ought to have been took straight off to the Union."

"I will take the responsibility of bringing her here, Pike," answered Lady Lucille. "I am not

afraid of my father being angry. He is more like
the good Samaritan than the Levite."

"In course, Lady Lucille; but you see in those
days there was no Unions; and a gentleman as
pays poor rates to the extent his lordship does
wouldn't lay himself out to have tramps brought
into his bedrooms and laid upon his beds."

"Will you go and get me that wine, Pike, before
this poor thing dies?" asked Lucille piteously;
whereupon Pike bolted, like an arrow from a bow.

The ever alert Miss Marjorum, not so deep in
Dante's *Inferno* as to be beyond earshot of mundane
voices, heard steps in the corridor, and came tripping out to discover what was happening. She saw
Pike's receding figure, and the half-open door of the
bedroom; and she flew to ascertain the cause of this
unwonted violation of the noontide stillness. Her
horror on beholding the figure on the bed, the limp
rag of gown or petticoat, the tattered shawl, the
bandaged bleeding foot, reduced her for the moment
to speechlessness. Then her loathing found words,
and she exclaimed,

"Lucille, in mercy's name, WHAT is that?" pointing to the bed.

"A poor girl I found in the wood—dying of
hunger and fatigue."

"My sweet pet, come away! Lady Lucille, come

away from her this instant!" shrieked the governess. "Look how dirty she is!"

"Her clothes are dusty, Marjy dear, that's all. Her poor face is not dirty. I daresay she tried to be clean, poor helpless thing."

"And you brought her here—yourself! This is too dreadful!"

Just then Pike appeared with a small tumbler of port, and a hunch of sponge-cake, on a silver salver.

"O Pike, Pike, how can you aid and abet your mistress in such dreadful goings on?" asked Miss Marjorum.

Lucille took the wine, tenderly lifted the tired head upon her arm, and put the glass to the white wan lips. The girl's eyes opened, and she drank a little wine with a choking sound like a sob; and then Lucille dipped the cake into the wine, and fed her, as she had often fed a young bird.

"Lucille, come away!" exclaimed Miss Marjorum, snatching the tumbler from her pupil's hand. "She may have some contagious disease—smallpox, perhaps."

"Look at her beautiful face, Marjy. Does that look like smallpox?"

"I don't know; but I insist upon your leaving this room. You may have escaped from the schoolroom, you may shirk Dante; but I hope I have still a shred of authority."

"Dearest Marjy, I will do anything in reason," said Lucille; while Miss Marjorum sternly administered the rest of the wine, with as severe an air as if she had been offering the fatal goblet of poison to a superfluous member of some royal Mussulman house. "All I want is that this poor thing may be cared for and made comfortable for the next few days."

"In this house?" demanded Miss Marjorum.

"Certainly. I shall be very angry with any one who talks of sending her out of this house," replied Lucille, with that air of authority which Lord Ingleshaw's only daughter very well knew how to assume upon occasion.

"I said from the first she ought to have been took to the Union," murmured Pike, looking deferentially from the governess to her pupil, hardly knowing which of the two he most feared.

"Of course; the Union is too good for such a low creature. Look at her feet; she must have tramped for days. She must be a professional beggar."

"She did not beg of me," said Lucille, ringing the bell. "You may go, Pike;" whereupon Pike pulled an imaginary forelock, and retired.

Lady Lucille's summons was answered promptly by her maid Tompion, who had been sitting at work in a room opening into the corridor.

"Tompion, I want you to take particular care of this young woman," said Lucille. "You will get her some soup immediately—a small cup of soup, for she has been a long time without food; and when she has eaten it, you will let her sleep as much as she likes for the next few hours. Then when she wakes you will get her a bath, and some clean linen out of my wardrobe, and one of my cotton gowns; and you will make her as comfortable as you possibly can. She is to occupy this room till she has recovered her strength, and by that time I shall have made up my mind what to do with her."

Tompion had not a word to oppose to the calm authority of these instructions. She was a strongly-built wholesome woman of about thirty, who had been Lucille's attendant since the departure of nurse and nursery-maid. She idolised her young mistress, and was devoted to her duties, although she would gladly have drawn the line at attendance upon dusty footsore tramps.

"I'm sure I don't know however I shall get them things off her, Lady Lucille," she said. "I expect they'll all drop to pieces when I touch 'em, like a 'Gyptian mummy."

"You must do your best, Tompion," said Lucille. "You are so kind-hearted that I know you'll be good to the poor thing."

"Lucille, *are* you coming away?" remonstrated Miss Marjorum.

Lucille put her arm round the governess's skinny shoulders, and left the room with her. Bess had fallen asleep after that half-tumbler of port and half-dozen mouthfuls of cake. It was more nourishment than she had had for the last three days.

"Lucille, you smell of tramps," said Miss Marjorum solemnly. "If you take my advice, you'll give yourself a warm bath before you resume the usual occupations of the day."

"I will take your advice, dear. That poor thing was dreadfully dusty. But is she not a lovely creature?"

"Her features may be well formed; but I cannot bring myself to see beauty in such abject degradation," replied the governess stiffly.

"Why degraded, Marjy? Only poor and friendless and hungry. I don't see any degradation in that. Think of Him who knew not where to lay His head."

This was attacking Jane Marjorum on her weakest and best side, for she was honestly religious.

"If I thought the girl were only poor, I would

not object to your helping her," she said; "but I fear she belongs to the criminal classes."

"But why, dear?"

"She looks like it," replied Miss Marjorum, not wishing to be explicit.

She had made up her mind that the girl was too pretty to be good.

———————

CHAPTER II.

MORE THAN KIN.

"And let me feel that warm breath here and there,
 To spread a rapture in my very hair.
 O, the sweetness of the pain!
 Give me those lips again!
 Enough! enough! It is enough for me
 To dream of thee."

LUCILLE had her bath, and dressed herself in the prettiest of pale-pink gingham gowns, trimmed with pillow-lace—that pretty old-fashioned thread-lace which gives employment to many a village child in the leafy lanes of Buckinghamshire—and appeared radiant before her old governess at their *tête-à-tête* luncheon. The Earl had gone to London by the eleven o'clock express. They had the Castle all to themselves, a stately abode of quietness and peace, the old pictured faces smiling at them, or seeming to smile, in the sunlight, just as in gloomy weather the same faces seemed to frown; the perfume of myriad flowers breathing in upon them through all the open casements.

They lunched in the old schoolroom, which served them as a breakfast or dining room when the Earl was away. Opening out of this was Lucille's morning-room—a white-panelled chamber, hung with water-colours, and much adorned with old china and new books. Here, in front of the wide low Tudor window, stood Lucille's grand piano, her father's gift on her seventeenth birthday; and across the ebony case was spread a tremendous work of art in the shape of a floral design on olive-green cloth, executed in gold and colours by the patient fingers of Miss Marjorum; and on this embroidered cloth stood a low, wide, green Venetian glass vase full of white azaleas and gardenias, an arrangement which satisfied all the requirements of high art.

Before Lucille sat down to luncheon, she was gratified by Tompion's assurance that the tramp had eaten her soup, and was "sleeping beautiful."

"Don't call her a tramp, Tompion," said Lucille; "her name is Bess. She may be no more accustomed to tramping than you or I. It may be only an accident in her life."

Tompion did not believe this; but was too well-trained a servant to argue, even with a mistress who had grown up to her hand.

Lucille laughed and talked gaily all luncheon-time. She was full of Bruno's return.

"What are we to do to amuse him, Marjy, now that there's no hunting or shooting?" she asked. "We must have tennis. Those girls from the Vicarage must be allowed to come every afternoon. And we must have picnics and excursionising of all kinds. I wonder whether my father would object to my learning to throw a fly? I should so like to go trout-fishing with Bruno."

Miss Marjorum held forth gravely on the impropriety of this suggestion.

"My dear Lucille, you really ought to remember that you might actually have been presented this season," she said; and this was her most solemn form of reproval.

"I am very glad I wasn't," answered the girl. "I am most grateful to his lordship for the year's reprieve."

"Most girls in your position would long to be out."

"I haven't the faintest longing. I daresay I shall enjoy society very well when I am in it; and I do long for the opera, to hear all the music I know so well upon the piano, sung by grand singers. Yes, that must be too delightful. But I don't suppose I shall ever be happier than I have been at Ingleshaw."

"My dear, however happy your lot may be, you will discover the hollowness of life," answered Miss Marjorum, winding up a very substantial lunch with cream cheese, spring radishes, and Bath Olivers. "We all do that as we advance in years."

"Dear Miss Marjorum, I hope your life has not been very hollow," said Lucille, wondering a little wherein the hollowness of such a life could lie; seeing that, for the last ten years, Jane Marjorum had lived upon the fat of the land, had been in receipt of a handsome salary, had been petted and made much of by her pupil, and most generously treated by the Earl; while her duties were ever of the lightest.

But Jane Marjorum was not taken aback by this question.

"I am of those who find out the hollowness of life before the bloom of youth has departed," she said, in a solemn voice. "I was engaged for five years to a young man whom I believed an apostle. I assisted him to keep his college terms at St. Catherine's, Cambridge (vulgarly called Cat's); and when he was ordained he proved hollow."

"In what way, Marjy?"

"He sent me back my letters and presents, and

told me that he should ever honour me as his friend and benefactress, but that Fate had willed that he was to fall in love with a milliner's apprentice at Cambridge, and that Duty impelled him to marry her. He is now rector of a parish in the East Riding, and that milliner's apprentice is on visiting terms with the county families," concluded Miss Marjorum, as if this were the crowning wrong. "So I think you will admit that *I* soon discovered the hollowness of life," she added, after a pause.

"It was very dishonourable of him," said Lucille, wondering whether the milliner's apprentice was pretty, and wondering a little also what kind of a person dear old Marjorum was in her day of freshness and bloom. She belonged to that section of the elderly whom it is almost impossible to imagine as ever having been young.

After luncheon Miss Marjorum again suggested the *Inferno;* but Lucille was in no mood for serious study. That idea of Bruno's return, added to her interest in her new *protégée*, completely filled her mind.

"It would be no use, Marjy dear," she said; "I should be only pretending to understand. I'll practise this afternoon; and you and I will go for a long walk after five-o'clock tea."

She went to her beloved piano, and played

Mozart's sonatas for the next two hours. It was music which she knew well, and which allowed her thoughts and fancies to wander fetterless.

Would he be much changed, this old companion of her childhood, she wondered, as her fingers ran over the airy passages of an *allegro* movement, in that neat delicate playing which is the result of much careful practice? Would he despise the simple pleasures of Ingleshaw?—the woods, the rural lanes, the meadows golden with buttercups, and flushed here and there with ruddy patches of wild sorrel; the hawthorn thickets where the thrushes sang so divinely at eventide; the old village church, whose old-fashioned homely services Lucille had attended all her life. Would all these things have lost their charm for him, now that he had seen every great city of Europe, steeping himself in the romance of a historical past, climbing Swiss mountains, fishing in Norwegian waters?

"He used to be very fond of the country," she told herself; "but I am afraid it will all seem very small to him after the wonders he has seen abroad."

Just before the eight-o'clock dinner Lady Lucille went to the room where the wanderer was lying. She found her much restored, but still very weak. Tompion had washed her, and put on clean linen;

and the perfect face upon the pillow looked all the more beautiful now the bronze-brown hair had been brushed, and was coiled in a loose plait at the back of the small head.

"How good you have been to me, lady!" she murmured softly, looking up with a grateful expression in her large dark eyes. "I did not think there was anybody in this world so good as you."

"Then I'm afraid you have never read the Gospel; for that would teach you that it is our duty to help the poor and friendless."

"I'm not much of a hand at reading, lady," the girl answered meekly. "I've forgot most what I was taught at the ragged school when I was a little un. There was ladies sometimes came down the alley where I lived, and they give me tracks, and says I must read 'em if I wanted to save my soul alive; but when I came in of a night, after tramping half over London with a basket of violets or moss-rose buds, I hadn't the strength left in me to tackle one of them there tracks, which allus led off by tellin' me I was goin' to hell."

"There is better teaching in the Gospel than in those tracts, Bess. The Gospel shows us the way to heaven. Would you like me to come and read to you a little before you compose yourself for the night?"

"Yes, lady, I should like you to come and sit by me a bit. I like to look at you, and to hear you talk; it ain't like anything as I've been used to. It's like waking up out of a bad dream and finding oneself in a new world. But you'll be for packing me off to-morrer, I dessay, sending me back to my parish, won't yer, lady?"

"No, no, you poor soul. You sha'n't leave the Castle till you are strong and well; and when you do go, I shall try to find you a comfortable home where you can get an honest living. We won't talk about it now; you are to think of nothing except getting well."

"I don't know that," answered the girl, with a plaintive look in the dark liquid eyes, "it might be better for me just to lie here till I die, and never know nothing more of life and its troubles."

"You shall find by and by that life is not all trouble; that there are a great many things in this world worth living for."

An hour later Lady Lucille came back and read some chapters from St. John's Gospel, but not before she had gently sounded the wanderer's religious knowledge. She found her wofully ignorant, her only ideas of gospel truth consisting of vague and patchy recollections of the New Testament as it had been expounded to her by a series of unsympathetic district visitors, so various in their views as to be eminently confusing in their teaching. Gently and briefly Lucille tried to bring before the girl's mind the grand and beautiful image of a Redeemer, before she read those chapters in which Christ reveals Himself and the fair hope of a blessed immortality to His disciples.

Bess listened intently, understanding not very much perhaps—the light as yet was but a faint glimmer—but deeply interested, soothed by the sweet voice of the reader, dazzled by that idea of a spiritual world which had never before been adequately presented to her imagination. She fell asleep with faint echoes of the Saviour's words floating in her half-awakened mind.

Lucille went to see her *protégée* early next morning. Bess was refreshed and strengthened by nourishing food and rest, and was eager to get up.

"If there was anything I could do for you, lady—" she began.

"Call me Lady Lucille; that is my name."

"Lady Lucille—that's a pretty name!—if there was anything I could do—but, Lord ha' mercy upon me! I'm such a hignorant creature, except to tramp about with a basket of flowers in spring and summer time, and to sell bootlaces or fusees in winter, I ain't good for nothink!"

"We will soon make you good for ever so many things. I am sure you are not stupid."

"Well, no, Lady Lu—Lucille, folks mostly says I'm sharp. I could turn my hand to pretty nigh anything, if I had the chance. I've sung ballads in the publics sometimes of a Saturday night: 'She wore a Wreath o' Roses,' and 'We met,' and 'The Last Rose o' Summer,' and suchlike."

"My maid shall teach you plain needlework. Are you clever with your needle?"

"Lord, no, Lady Lucille! I never could lay hold on a needle proper. It allus slips through my fingers."

"You will very soon learn. Every woman ought to be clever at needlework. The taste is born with us, I think. But the first thing I want to teach you is to pray. Perhaps, though you know so little of the Gospel, you have been taught to say your prayers?"

"No, Lady Lucille; them I lived among didn't hold with praying. 'What should we be the better for craw-thumping and squalling hymns?' I've heard 'em say. 'That wouldn't get us a meal o' victuals.'"

"Poor souls! they did not know how Christ

taught us to ask our Father for all good things. Our prayers may not always be answered just as we wish, or as soon as we want; but we know they are always heard, and that God gives us what is best for us."

"I dessay if I lived in this house I should believe that," said Bess, to whom the plainest bed-chamber in Ingleshaw Castle was like an arbour in the Garden of Eden.

Lucille taught her to repeat the Lord's Prayer, and one of those ejaculatory verses in the Psalms, which, after that one sublime supplication, are of all prayers the simplest and the best. It was slow work to teach one who had never been taught anything since those dim half-forgotten days when the ragamuffin child had been one among a herd of other ragamuffins in a ragged school; but Lucille was accustomed to the density of the agricultural mind, and she found an acuteness of intellect in this child of London slums and alleys which promised rapid progress in the future.

To her maid Tompion Lady Lucille intrusted the task of teaching this city waif the art of plain needlework, and the simplest household duties.

"If she really feels strong enough to get up by and by, you can show her how to arrange her room; and then, after she has had her dinner in the ser-

vants' hall"—Tompion's jaw fell, doubtful how even
the lower house in the servants' hall would brook
the introduction of this vagabond damsel—"you can
teach her a little plain sewing."

Tompion followed her mistress into the corridor.

"You don't mean to keep her at the Castle, do
you, Lady Lucille," she inquired, "a young person
without a character?"

"We shall find out what her character is in a
few days."

"Just consider, Lady Lucille, she may be mixed
up with burglars! What will his lordship say?"

"That is my business, Tompion. You may be
sure I shall not keep her here without his lordship's permission. I may get her a place in the
neighbourhood. What you have to do is to teach
her to be a handy little maid."

"It ain't so easy to teach a tramp that has
never been used to decent ways," muttered the reluctant Tompion.

"You will find her very clever and teachable.
Her wits have been sharpened in the school of ad-
versity. This is the first time I have ever asked
you to do anything out of the beaten track, Tompion.
I hope you are not going to be disagreeable about it."

Tompion vowed that she would not shrink from
going through fire and water for her mistress, much

less would she refuse to teach a characterless young female, whose habits no doubt were dirty, and whose language must needs be improper.

Lucille and Miss Marjorum spent a studious morning, deep in Dante's *Inferno*, the girl's eager mind leaping all grammatical fences, and seizing the spirit of the poet, the vivid dramatic power of the scene; the patient governess arresting her at every line to expatiate upon tenses and cases, relatives and predicates, with that affection for dry detail which is the favourite virtue of all mediocre teachers. The weather to-day was less distractingly lovely. The sky wore its sober English gray; and Lucille was content to stay indoors till the afternoon constitutional walk or drive which she was in the habit of taking with her governess.

Would Bruno come to-day? No, that was hardly possible. His rooms were ready; Lucille had herself been to look at them; a charming suite of rooms in the north wing, near the Earl's own quarters. Lucille had arranged the hot-house flowers on tables and mantelshelf; and her own hands had composed those still lovelier groups of field and woodland blossoms in low vases of dark dull green Venetian glass. She wanted him to be struck with the beauty of Ingleshaw, even after Italy.

After luncheon she went to see what progress

Bess was making in Tompion's care. She found
the damsel sitting by an open window, clothed in
one of Tompion's neat cotton gowns, with her brown
hair bound up in a classic knot, and set off by one
of Tompion's somewhat coquettish muslin caps. Her
attire was neatness itself; and the beauty, which
had been striking even in dusty rags, had been
made all the more brilliant by soap-and-water and
clean raiment. Lucille felt proud of having picked
up such a gem by the wayside.

Bess rose at the young lady's entrance, blushing
and sparkling at sight of her benefactress. Tompion
had been discoursing largely on her mistress's im-
portance, on the lofty height from which she had
stooped to raise a fallen fellow-creature from the
dust. The good Samaritan was an estimable person,
no doubt; but he belonged to a despised race, and
was perhaps a nobody. Here, on the contrary,
was the daughter and heiress of an English nobleman, whose earldom dated from the Tudors, a
damsel born in the purple and ermine of life, and
in whose person charity must be a virtue of sur-
passing beauty. Bess, holding her needle clumsily,
cobbled her seam industriously, and listened meekly
to Tompion's holding forth. Slight as was her
knowledge of any world above the wilderness of
courts and back slums in which she had been bred,

Bess was quite shrewd enough to know that a young lady living in such a house as Ingleshaw Castle must needs belong to the elect of this earth.

Tompion, who loved to talk, had told the waif all that could be told about Ingleshaw and its inhabitants. She told her how Mr. Challoner, her young lady's kinsman and old playfellow, was expected on a visit, after his tour in the south of Europe. The south of Europe was only a sound to Bess, whose geographical knowledge was nil; but she was keenly interested in the idea of a young man who, if he had not exactly "kept company" with her benefactress in the past, was very likely to keep company with her in the future.

"It's pretty well known that his lordship would like them to marry," said Tompion, with authority. "It would keep the estates together, don't you see; for there's a good deal that doesn't go with the title, and that will belong to Lady Lucille by and by. And his lordship is very fond of Mr. Challoner."

"Is he a good-looking young chap?" inquired Bess.

"He's a handsome fine-grown young gentleman. You mustn't call him a chap. It's a very vulgar word."

"I knows a many that's a deal vulgarer," said

4*

Bess. "Lor's, if you thinks chap vulgar, I could say words as would make your hair stand on end!"

"But you must forget those horrid words. If you want Lady Lucille to be kind to you, and to take an interest in you, you must try to be genteel, like me."

"O, you're genteel, are you?" asked the homeless one, with a mocking tone, which Miss Tompion disliked exceedingly. "You're the pattern I'm to cut myself out upon? I'd rather look higher, and imitate Lady Lucille."

"You're an ungrateful impertinent young woman!" exclaimed Tompion indignantly; "and if I hadn't promised my lady, I'd wash my hands of you this instant. But Lady Lucille begged of me as a favour to teach you proper behaviour and plain sewing, and I'll do my best to oblige her."

"I ax your pardon," said Bess, the mischievous light in her splendid eyes softening to meekness as she spoke; "I didn't mean to be rude. I'll do anything, or learn anything, Lady Lucille wishes; but I thought if I was to copy any one I might as well copy her."

"That's too absurd!" exclaimed Tompion, just as Lucille entered. "Copy her, indeed!"

Her presence seemed to fill the room with sunshine, Bess thought; and when she spoke kindly

and praised her *protégée's* neat appearance, the dark
eyes filled with grateful tears.

"You are ever so much better, are you not?"
asked Lucille.

"Pretty nigh well, my lady; only a little weak
and tottery like. I shall be all right to-morrow;
and if you want me to go on to Dover, why, I can
do it."

"That depends upon what your Dover friends
could do for you."

"It won't be much, my lady," answered the girl,
with a despondent look. "The friend I've got there
is—only—a kind of a cousin, a young man as lived
in the same alley. He talked of 'listing for a
soldier, and I heard tell as he'd gone to Dover;
but I don't know for certain as he's there."

"You must not think of going after him," said
Lucille. "What could he do for you, poor fellow—
a soldier, without a friend in the place? You shall
stop in this house till I get you a situation of some
kind. And now come with me, and I'll show you
the pictures. That will cheer you and amuse you,
for you don't look strong enough to do much work
yet. Can you walk a little?"

"Anywheres with you, Lady Lucille."

Lucille took her through those pretty quaint old
rooms, showed her the pictures and cabinets of

china, which so many tourists came to see, and was
infinitely amused by her curious exclamations and
remarks, her utter ignorance, as of a child of three
or four years old.　There was much that might be
taught her while she was looking at the pictures;
passages of sacred history, the names of historic
personages, great events in the past.　Her mind
was a blank; but she was eager to receive information, and showed a keen interest in those pictured
scenes, and all that Lucille could tell her about
them.

Then Lucille took her in hand, and began the
laborious work of revising a form of the English
language which had been acquired in Whitechapel,
and enriched with the copious slang of London low
life—the varieties of provincial dialect picked up
in that cosmopolitan city where Bess had been
reared.　She had an intuitive knowledge of her
own lowness, and a perfect willingness to have her
speech refined and purified by her benefactress.

Finally, Lucille showed the girl her own rooms;
and these seemed to Bess even more exquisite than
those stately panelled and pictured apartments
which were shown to tourists.

All the minute elegances of a girl's surroundings
—the books and flowers, statuettes and water-
coloured drawings, the piano, the high-art glass and

pottery, Japanese lacquer, South Kensington tapes-
tries—formed one brilliant whole, which dazzled
and enchanted the eyes that had only seen art and
luxury through the shop-windows, while standing
weary and sick at heart on the muddy pavement
outside. Miss Marjorum, sitting at her crewel-work
frame in the recess of a window, acknowledged
Bess's curtsy with the most formal bend of which
her back, long trained to formality, was capable.
She did not approve of this girl's introduction into
the Castle, and she was longing for the Earl's return, which she anticipated would put a speedy
end to Lucille's folly. She most strongly disapproved of the girl's appearance in these rooms,
where her trained eyes were no doubt taking in
every detail of windows and shutters, bolts and
locks, for the future use of those burglars with
whom Miss Marjorum, like Tompion, believed the
damsel to be in association. All such wandering
damsels were doubtless more or less the companions
and accomplices of thieves. And then, again, the
prettiness of the creature, in which even Miss Marjorum's coldly critical eye could see no flaw, was
one of those objectionable features in the case
which could not be reasoned away. Such a being,
born and cradled in the gutter, bore in her own
breast the star of an inevitable destiny.

Lucille spent an hour in displaying the glories of Ingleshaw to her *protégée*, charmed with the girl's intense appreciation of every beautiful thing which she saw; an appreciation which was not the less real because it was expressed in a language common to costermongers and their families. To teach her a new and more refined mode of speech was the first task which Lucille set herself, and, in order to bring about this result, Bess must first learn to read; so Lucille appointed the next morning for a reading-lesson, Tompion, in the mean while, being charged to carry on the refining process by all means in her power.

Lucille devoted two hours after breakfast to this first reading-lesson. She found that Bess knew her letters, and had a vague glimmering of acquaintance with the easier monosyllables in the English language; but it was very much like beginning at the beginning. Lucille's patience was inexhaustible, and the pupil's intellect as keen as a razor; so a great deal was done in those two hours, more being effected by oral instruction, by the refining process of intercourse with a cultivated mind, than by the mere spelling out words upon the page of a primer.

Miss Marjorum held herself altogether aloof from this initiatory lesson. She would gladly have taken all the trouble of Bess's education on her hands had she approved Lucille's scheme; but she would not have any part in an affair which she considered to the last degree imprudent and hazardous.

"My dear, I think you know I am not one to spare my own trouble," she said, when Lucille came to the schoolroom, having left Bess to learn the mystery of an under-housemaid's work from Tompion; "but I cannot go with you in this matter. I feel that harm will come of it."

Lucille knew her old governess too well to attempt an argument. She stopped her dear Marjorum's mouth with Dante; and they went down to the third circle, and floundered there till luncheon.

After luncheon came rainy weather, so Marjorum retired to her room to read a dryasdust biography of a New Zealand missionary, just received from Mudie. Lucille strongly suspected that Marjorum's readings in retirement were only another name for sleep. Pleased to be alone, the girl sat down to her beloved Mozart, and lost herself in a maze of melody, in which, somehow or other, Bruno was always entangled.

She had been thinking of him so much that it was hardly a surprise when the door opened softly just as she was singing "Batti, batti," and he came into the room.

"Don't stop!" he cried, as she rose from the piano; "go on, Lucie. It is like hearing you talk to me. How are you, dear?" he asked, coming over to her and seating himself at her side; and then in a rich baritone he took up the pleading tender melody. "O Lucie, if you knew how glad I am to be home again!" he said, at the end of the phrase.

"Glad to come back from Italy, the country every one sighs to visit!" she exclaimed, her face radiant with delight. "I was afraid you would despise Ingleshaw, after all the lovely places you have seen."

"The places I have seen are passing lovely; but there's not one of them to compare with the gray towers and green woods of Ingleshaw, in my mind, Lucie. Of course you expected me after my telegram?"

"I have been expecting you every moment, though I suppose it was a physical impossibility that you could come before now?"

"Well, yes, unless I had come in a balloon. They tell me his Lordship is in London."

"Yes; there was some important division; but he will be home in a day or two, I hope."

"And in the mean time I am your guest."

"Yes, and I am forgetting my duties as a

hostess. You must be hungry or thirsty, after your journey. Let me order luncheon for you."

"No, dear. I lunched at the Charing Cross Hotel. I have no such low wants as meat or drink. I want to look at you, to talk to you, to see what change the last two years have made in you."

"Do you find me very much altered?" asked Lucille, her eyelids drooping under the ardent admiration of his gaze.

"Not altered. The bud does not alter when it blossoms into the rose. My bud has blossomed, that is all. And you are not to make your *début* this season, Lucie? I am so glad of that."

"Why, Bruno?"

"Because I shall have you all to myself. You and I will drain the cup of bliss as it is brewed at Ingleshaw. We will be children again. We will picnic, we will light fires and boil tea-kettles, we'll revel in blackberry-hunting, nutting, mushroom-gathering. I have half a mind to resume the manufacture of daisy-chains. It is almost exciting, for the stalks are so liable to give way at critical moments."

"My father says you are to go into Parliament, and become a great politician."

"Oh, I know I am an embryo Canning; but I mean to enjoy the embryo stage as long as I can.

You shall help me. We'll read blue-books together. Hansard is intensely interesting to right-minded people whose brains are not soddened by novels and poetry."

"I should be so proud if I could help you."

"If you could? You can; you shall. You shall be my Egeria; and between us we will do as much good for England as Numa did for Rome."

"Ah, Bruno, if you can find some good way of helping the poor, how proud I shall be of your political career!" said Lucie, thinking of that weed from the waste of Whitechapel which she was eager to cultivate into a flower. "There is a poor girl in this house—a creature whom I found in the plantation almost dying—and she has opened my eyes to the sad state of things among the London poor."

"Ah, my dearest child, that is an old canker. Heaven knows how legislation is to find a cure for it! The favourite panacea of the present day is education; perhaps the coming idea may be food. When we have failed in the cultivation of sound minds in half-starved bodies, we may try again, and begin at the other end. And so you rescued some poor dying girl, and brought her home to your own house? That sounds quixotic."

"O Bruno, if we were all a little more like Don Quixote, the world might be better than it is."

"True, dearest; the sweetest natures are those of the people who are oftenest taken in."

"Would you like to see her?"

"Her? Who?" asked Bruno vaguely, his eyes dwelling on the fair young face in which every beauty had developed within the period of his absence. Not easy were it to imagine a fairer picture than these two sitting side by side in the calm afternoon light—the young man tall, broad-shouldered, with dark complexion and strongly-marked features, eyes of that sombre brown which seems the natural hue of thought, but just now with a smile of much sweetness lighting up his face; Lucille, delicately fair, with eyes of limpid blue, and exquisitely chiselled features, a thoroughly patrician beauty—the two looking at each other with such happy trustfulness, two souls that were not afraid of betraying their perfect union.

"My poor girl. Her name is Bess; she has not told me her surname. I am doubtful if she has ever known one, and I don't like to ask her awkward questions."

"Don Quixote is nowhere in the scale of chivalry, compared with you," said Bruno, smiling at her.

"Would you like to see her?"

"Not the faintest objection. I don't mind look-

ing on at a procession of surnameless damsels, so
long as you stay and look on with me."

"I want you to see her, for I know you are a
judge of character. Dear old Marjorum has been
so disagreeable about her—calls me imprudent for
giving her shelter; vows that harm will come of it;
and both she and Tompion talked about burglars,
just as if all poor people were thieves."

"I'm afraid I should justify that idea if I were
houseless and starving. I should make my poor
little effort towards bringing about universal equality
in the financial line. And so dear old Marjorum
thinks you have picked up a she-burglar, and
trembles for the safety of the family plate?"

"She is so dreadfully prejudiced," said Lucille,
ringing the bell.

She told the tall and powdered youth who attended that the young person in Tompion's charge
was to bring in the afternoon tea. This was
Tompion's special duty, her young mistress preferring the ministration of her own maid at this
unceremonious meal to the statelier attendance of
butler or footman; and Tompion bristled with in-
dignation on receiving the powdered youth's mes-
sage. But she dared not disobey.

Bruno had forgotten the existence of his cousin's

protégée before the tea was brought; he had so much to say to Lucille after their long separation, so much to tell her, so many questions to ask.

"You must have enjoyed yourself immensely," said Lucille, listening open-eyed to a rapid account of rambles from Rome to Madrid; from Dresden to Odessa; a bewildering confusion of catacombs, Escurial, royal picture-galleries, Tyrolese mountain and woodland, Danube, Prado, Norwegian fisheries, Roman Carnival. "You seem to have seen everything; but I think you must have travelled rather in the style of those American tourists one reads about. Confess, now, that you scampered," said Lucille.

"If I did, it was that I might come home to you all the sooner," replied Bruno.

The door was thrown open by the powdered youth, with that grand air which distinguishes the thoroughbred footman from the promoted knife-boy. With the same broad dignity of action the tall youth brought forward a Chippendale tea-table, and unfolded its inlaid leaves before his mistress, just in time to receive the circular Japanese tea-tray which Bess, shy, and with downcast eyelids, carried into the room.

Bruno looked up at her, first with a kindly

interest, and then with undisguised admiration.
Perhaps in all his life he had never seen such perfect beauty—not in marble or on canvas in all
those art-galleries where he had feasted upon ideal
beauty to satiety during the last two years. The
face was not more perfect, perhaps, than those
idealised models of the old painters and sculptors;
only it was alive: a living, radiant, vivid beauty,
blushing, tremulous, with the shy sweet sense of its
own power.

For a novice in the ways of civilisation, Bess
performed the duties of her situation admirably. A
clever girl, whose wits have been sharpened by
semi-starvation, can learn anything which is a mere
matter of eye and hand. Bess handed the porcelain
cups and silver cream-ewer as deftly as if she
had been handling porcelain and silver all her life.
There was no uncouthness in her movements.
Lucille detained her as long as she reasonably
could, anxious that Bruno should have leisure for
observation. They talked only of the lightest topics
while she waited upon them; and that light airy
talk seemed to Bess like a new language. Every
word, every intonation, was different from the words
and tones to which she had been accustomed. To
her ear, naturally delicate, that refined speech had
almost the charm of music. She drank in every

tone; and as she looked at Bruno Challoner, mentally comparing that tall strong frame, those finely-cut definite features, and the dark thoughtful eyes, with the wizened stunted undergrowth, or burly and bloated overgrowth, of the companions of her youth, the crafty mouth, the ferret eyes, this man appeared to her as a grand and godlike creature, the inhabitant of an unknown world.

"Now for your opinion," said Lucille eagerly, when Bess had left the room with the tea-tray. "Do you think I have done a very dreadful thing in befriending that poor creature?"

"Indeed no, dear. I don't see any sign of the burglarious temperament," answered Bruno, smiling at his cousin's earnest face; "but at the same time it may be rather difficult to know what to do with your *protégée*. We must ask his lordship's advice. I don't think you ought to keep her in the Castle, since you know nothing whatever of her antecedents; and, after all, the Ingleshaw plate-room, or even your own jewel-cases, might be a temptation."

"O Bruno, when you have just seen her sweet innocent face!"

"Not to her, perhaps, but to her friends," said Bruno apologetically. "No young woman can grow up, in any sphere of life, without having friends,

don't you know. Perhaps the best thing you could
do for this girl would be to apprentice her to some
country dressmaker—at Sevenoaks or Tunbridge,
for instance; and if she behave well during her ap-
prenticeship you might get one of your friends to
engage her as a lady's-maid. I should think that
must be better than being a journeywoman dressmaker."

"What I should like to do is to keep her in the
Castle. She could help Tompion in some light kind
of work. This morning I began to teach her to
read; she is horribly ignorant, but so bright and
quick that it is a pleasure to teach her."

"That would be all very well, if you knew her
antecedents; but, as you don't—"

"I have not asked her any questions about her
past life; she was so weak and ill when I brought
her home. I want her to feel assured of my kindness before I question her."

"And when you do she may favour you with
one of those romances which people in her position
are quite capable of inventing. I don't want to dis-
hearten you, dear, in your effort to do a good work:
but this is a matter in which I think you ought to
be ruled by your father's wisdom and experience."

"Then I'm sure I shall have my own way," said

Lucille, with a radiant smile. "My father never denies me anything."

After this they talked of themselves, and Bess was forgotten. Miss Marjorum came in presently—the Maori missionary having proved peculiarly interesting this gray drowsy afternoon—and was intensely surprised to find Bruno established in the morning-room. They dined together; and after dinner Bruno and Lucille went for a moonlight ramble in the park; a ramble about which Miss Marjorum had some qualms of conscience, lest it might be considered a breach of that severe etiquette to which her soul inclined. Two years ago the cousins had wandered together at their own will; for in those days Lucille was counted as a child; but now Lucille was a woman, and the line must be drawn somewhere. Ought it not to be drawn at moonlit rambles? Happily the Earl would be home to-morrow; and this delicate question might be submitted to him.

Lord Ingleshaw did not return next day. A letter came for Lucille, telling her that the business in the Lords had hung fire, and that he would have to stay in Grosvenor-square a few days longer, so as to be ready with his vote. Lucille was to take care of Bruno, and to keep him at the Castle till her father's return.

Lucille found no difficulty in obeying these instructions. Bruno found the summer days only too short in his cousin's company. Poor Miss Marjorum, always bent upon adhering as nearly as she could to her own severe code of etiquette, drove and walked with them in the broiling sun and the treacherous wind until her nose was blistered in the service. But Marjorum's presence was to them as if it had not been. They were as loving as Romeo and Juliet under her very nose; and there were times when, in these long rustic rambles, Marjorum was fain to sit down on some green bank by the wayside, sheltered by overhanging hawthorn and blackberry, while Bruno and Lucille had the world all to themselves.

In one of these brief excursions into Paradise the young man caught his cousin suddenly in his arms, among the dancing lights and flickering shadows, under the luminous green of young beech leaves, and held the fair young face upon his breast while he bent to kiss those innocent lips, pleading for the right to call his dearest by a nearer and dearer name than cousin—calling her in advance, in the rapture of that passionate moment, bride and wife.

"Shall it not be so, love? It is the dream of my life!" he said.

"And of mine," she answered.

Then after a brief pause, in which they stood silent, lost in a happy dreamland, she said,

"Will my father be angry, Bruno, do you think? I would sooner die than disobey him."

"Dearest, I have some reason to believe your father will be glad."

"Then all the world is full of happiness," said Lucille; and then, clasping her lover's arm with a sudden impulse, she exclaimed, "O Bruno, let us be kind to the poor! God has been so good to us —so good! And when I think how many unhappy people there are in the world, while—"

"While our lives are steeped in bliss. Yes, it does seem hard, does it not, Lucie? 'There's something in this world amiss, shall be unriddled by and by.' That 'by and by' must seem such a long way off to those who suffer keenly to-day."

They went back to the lane where Miss Marjorum was nodding in a placid after-luncheon nap under the shelter of blackberry and hawthorn. They both looked so radiant that the spinster's keen eye divined something out of the common.

"Why, what mischief have you two been plotting?" she asked.

"Only to set village bells ringing before the

blackberries are ripe," said Bruno, laughing. "Marjy, you will have to give me a wedding-present. Please don't let it be a Bible or a Church-service, for I am handsomely provided with both."

———

CHAPTER III.

FROM SUNSHINE TO GLOOM.

"Who hath not felt that breath in the air,
  A perfume and freshness strange and rare,
A warmth in the light, and a bliss everywhere,
  When young hearts yearn together?"

FOR three days of unbroken unspeakable bliss
the lovers dreamed their fond and happy dream.
There was not a cloudlet on the brightness of their
sky. The very weather seemed made on purpose
for them. Never had the chase, or the plantations,
the rustic Kentish villages with their quaint old-
world air, the ruined abbey with its neatly-kept
gardens, and trim mansion-house hard by, the lanes,
the meadows, the river—never had that fair English
scenery, amidst which Lucille had been born and
bred, worn a lovelier aspect. She and Bruno walked
and rode and drove and idled about all through
the summery days. Except for that one hour which
she devoted every morning to the patient instruction
of Bess, Lucille's life was entirely absorbed by her
lover. Miss Marjorum felt that the bow must be

relaxed a little in favour of lovers newly engaged.
She was hourly expecting the Earl's return; and
then things would fall into a more orderly course.

On the third evening after that exchange of
vows in the little wood at the end of the blackberry lane, Lucille sat at her piano, with her lover
by her side. She was silent, softly playing a plaintive reverie by Gounod: and it seemed to Bruno
that for the last half-hour a strange seriousness had
come down upon her. He could hardly see her
face in the light of the low shaded lamp, but he
could see that she was very pale.

"I am afraid you are tired, Lucille," he said.

"Rather tired. Perhaps we rode a little too far
this afternoon."

"Not so far as yesterday, sweet."

"It must have been warmer to-day, then. I feel
ever so much more tired. I have a slight sore
throat. Don't look alarmed, Bruno: it will be well
to-morrow, I have no doubt."

"Are you subject to sore throat?"

"No, I don't remember having one for ages."

Bruno got up and rang the bell. Miss Marjorum
was writing letters at a distant table. She kept up
tremendous correspondences with the friends of her
youth—chiefly of the governess profession—and had
a vague but comfortable idea that her letters would

be published after her death, and would rank with the compositions of Mrs. Carter.

Bruno stopped to say a few words to her on his way to the piano. He begged her to send instantly for the family doctor. He had come from Italy, the land of fever, and was quick to take alarm at the faintest symptom of mischief.

He went back to his seat by Lucille. The girl had been playing all the time, dwelling with a lingering *legato* touch upon the tender dreamy music.

"Is there anything wrong?" she asked, seeing her old governess confabulating in a somewhat mysterious way with the footman who answered the bell.

"No, dear; but I know you are more tired than you confess, and I want you to go to bed very early and nurse that sore throat. O, by the bye, talking of your *protégée*"—of whom they had not been talking—"was there anything the matter with her when you found her in the plantation? I mean, anything beyond weakness and hunger? Was she in a fever?"

"O no," answered Lucille; "she had been laid up with a fever at the Union, and she was discharged as cured; but having no money and no friends, she wandered about in a starving condition till she fell helpless by the wayside."

"I see. She had a fever, and had been cured and discharged," said Bruno, with a terrible sinking at his heart.

He went back to Miss Marjorum, who had laid aside her letter, in the middle of a Johnsonian paragraph, and closed her desk, and who looked the image of trouble. He urged her to get Lucille to her room as soon as possible, but on no account to alarm her. But Lucille's quick mind had divined her lover's fears.

She rose from the piano, shivering and faint, and with an inward conviction that she was going to be ill—she whose brief happy life had been almost free from malady. She went over to Bruno and laid her hand gently on his shoulder, and drew him into the recess of the window, beyond Miss Marjorum's hearing.

"If I should have caught a fever from that poor thing, don't let her be sent away while I am ill," she pleaded earnestly.

"My dearest, it will not be in my power—" he began.

"It is the first favour I have asked you since our engagement, Bruno. Promise," she urged.

"I promise, love. I will do my uttermost to prevent her being sent away."

"It is not her fault, remember, dear. She did not know that the fever was contagious. She had been told that she was cured."

"Of course, dear. And who says you are going to have a fever?" said Bruno, pretending to be intensely cheerful. "You are only a little tired with our rides and rambles in the sunshine. If you go to bed early, and let Marjorum nurse you, I daresay you will be quite well to-morrow morning."

But Lucille was no better next morning—a great deal worse, rather; and on his early visit, before nine o'clock, the family doctor pronounced it a clearly marked case of scarlet fever. He saw Bess, and discovered that she was only just escaping from the most contagious condition of a convalescent patient, and that, when Lady Lucille took her home to the Castle, that dangerous condition must have been in full force. Tompion and Miss Marjorum had both had scarlet fever; but the carefully guarded Lucille had escaped the disease hitherto, and was a ready subject for contagion.

When Bess heard what had happened she was in an agony of grief. Mr. Wharton, the kind-hearted doctor, was constrained to comfort her by the assurance that at present there was no indication of danger.

"But at the same time," said Miss Marjorum severely, "I must say it was a very cruel act of you to come into this house, and bring trouble and sickness with you."

"I had better go away this minute," said Bess, drying her tears, and drawing herself up with more dignity of gesture than might be expected of a girl who had sold violets for a penny a bunch; "but you may bear in mind, lady, that I was brought into this house by that sweet angel when I hardly knew whether I was alive or dead, and that it was by her wish I stopped here. As to bringing sickness and trouble—well, what should such as I bring with me but trouble, that has never knowed anything else? But I'll go this moment. I can go on the tramp again, and fall back into all the old ways; but I can never forget the dear young lady that's ill. She was the first lady that ever treated me as if I was made of the same flesh and blood as herself."

"No, you are not to go away," said Bruno firmly. "It was Lady Lucille's special request to me that you should not be sent away while she was ill. Tompion, you will look after this young person during your lady's illness, and you will see that she learns to make herself useful."

Bess looked at Mr. Challoner with wide-open wondering eyes. It was the first time this godlike personage had spoken directly to her. His voice thrilled her; his eyes, with their steady divinely truthful look, awed her into silence. She stood before him as before a supernaturally gifted judge, who could read her secret thoughts.

"Yes," muttered Tompion, as Mr. Challoner left the room; "and she will go about the house giving other people fevers, I'll warrant! I don't know but what I've got the fever upon me myself. There's a many that have it twice."

"You needn't be afraid," said Mr. Wharton. "I'll take care that there shall be no risk of further infection, if this young person will do what I tell her."

"I'll do anything, sir," answered Bess meekly, her eyes still fixed on the doorway through which Bruno had gone. "I'd give half my life if they'd let me nurse that dear young lady."

"Why, what can you know of nursing, young woman?" asked the doctor.

"Poor folks has to help one another, sir," answered the girl meekly. "Many's the night I've sat up to nurse a neighbour, or a neighbour's child. We all lived so scrooged together down our court, one couldn't help being friendly."

"Yes, I know how good the poor are to the poor," said the doctor kindly. "Well, Mr. Challoner says you are to stay. We'll see, by and by, if you can be handy in the sick-room; but we must have better help than yours. I have telegraphed for a couple of nurses from an institution in London."

And now came all those dismal signs and tokens of an infectious illness which send a chill to the hearts of those who can only watch and wait for the result. Lady Lucille's rooms were cut off from all direct communication with the rest of the house. Sheets steeped in diluted carbolic acid hung before the doors. A nursing sister, in a prim black gown and a picturesque white cap, emerged solemnly at intervals to receive the various necessaries for the sick-room. Bruno was forbidden all access to his cousin's apartment, albeit he had had scarlet fever, and had no fear of infection. Miss Marjorum had suffered the malady in her infancy, and had an idea that the lapse of time had prepared her for a second attack; so, although deeply anxious about her pupil, she readily submitted to the decree of banishment.

To Bruno banishment seemed almost as hard to bear as it was to Romeo in the morning of his love. It was so hard to be parted from his betrothed in the very beginning of their engagement; to be so near her, and yet to be forbidden to see her, to clasp the dear hand, to whisper tender words of comfort and pity; hardest of all to know that while he walked about and chafed and fretted, in all the fulness of health and vigour, she lay prostrate and suffering, consumed with fever, the lips he kissed yesterday parched and pale, the sweet eyes dull and heavy.

He spent the greater part of the day pacing the garden-paths below Lady Lucille's rooms, looking up at the open windows, longing to hear his darling's voice, going into the house every half-hour to get the latest news of the sick-room. She was very ill, they told him, suffering a good deal from sore throat; but this was only natural. The disease must take its course.

The same train which brought the two nursing sisters brought Lord Ingleshaw, summoned by a telegram from Miss Marjorum. He had arranged to arrive at Ingleshaw on this day, and had looked forward to a joyful meeting with Bruno, who had written to tell him how Lucille and he only waited her father's approval of their engagement to make them completely happy. Bruno knew very well that to ask his kinsman's consent was only a respectful formula; enough had been said by the Earl in the past to assure him that Lord Ingleshaw had no dearer hope than to see his daughter married to her cousin.

But now, instead of meeting in joy, the Earl and his heir met in sorrow. True that the family doctor declared that the malady showed no sign of danger; that there was not even occasion for a second opinion. The fact that the bright happy girl lay prostrate and fever-stricken was full of pain and fear for those who so fondly loved her.

"How, in Heaven's name, can she have caught this fever?" asked the Earl, looking from Bruno to Miss Marjorum. "Where has she been? What has she been doing? Is there scarlet fever in the village? Has she been visiting any sick people?"

"I regret to say that the dear child's wilfulness is the sole cause of this misfortune," said Miss Marjorum; and then she proceeded to tell the story of Lucille's unconscious imitation of the good Samaritan.

The Earl was a Christian, deeply and earnestly religious; yet his first thought, on hearing the story, was that his daughter had acted like a fool. There is such a wide distance between mechanical benevolence—as shown in liberal contributions to all respectable charities, in large doles of bread and fuel dealt out by hireling hands—and in this personal practical compassion, which brings a patricians's daughter face to face with the child of the gutter.

Lord Ingleshaw's second thought was vindictive towards Bess.

"What has become of this girl? She has been sent away, of course?" he said.

"I regret to say that she has not," replied Miss Marjorum, with a crushing look at Bruno.

"Lucille earnestly entreated me last night that the young woman should not be sent away," said Bruno, unabashed. "I promised her that if it were in my power to prevent it she should not be sent away. She can do no further harm by remaining here."

"She can only rob the house, and murder us all in our beds," said Miss Majorum.

"His lordship can see her, and judge for himself what inclination she may have that way," replied Bruno.

"I'll see my daughter first," said Lord Ingle-shaw.

"My dear sir, consider: at your age scarlet fever might be fatal," exclaimed Miss Marjorum.

"I believe I have had scarlet fever. At any rate I have no fear of infection," answered the Earl.

"They won't let me see her," said Bruno piteously. "How I wish I might go with you!"

Unhappily, Mr. Wharton had expressly ordered that his patient was to be kept as quiet as possible, and was to see no one but her nurses. The father's authority overruled the doctor's; but there could be no such exception made in Bruno's favour. He had to content himself with pouring out his love and devotion in a hurried letter, which the Earl promised to give to Lucille.

Lord Ingleshaw stayed with his darling for about ten minutes, the day nurse looking grudgingly on at his caresses, as if he were poisoning her patient. Lucille was feeble and feverish, but her eyes brimmed over with joyful tears at sight of the dear father. She put her arms round his neck and hugged him, as he bent over her pillow.

"I'm afraid this is very agitating for her," murmured the nurse.

"No, no, indeed, father; don't go away yet. It does me a world of good to see you."

Before Lord Ingleshaw left her bedside he had promised that Bess should not be sent away. The mischief that was done could not be undone; and he could not steel himself against his sick child's tender pleading.

He sent for Bess, and saw her alone in the library; the girl deeply awed by the grave yet splendid aspect of the room—the walls of books, the carved oak cabinets, the massive writing-table, before which the Earl sat in his large crimson morocco-covered armchair, an imposing figure, with fine intellectual face, and silvered hair and beard.

He questioned her closely, as it would never have occurred to Lady Lucille to question her, and this was the utmost he could obtain from her:

She could remember neither father nor mother. She had been brought up by an old woman, who went hawking in town and country, sometimes selling one kind of goods, sometimes another— flowers and fruit mostly in London, lace and haberdashery in the country. The woman treated her badly, beat her, and half-starved her, and as soon as she was old enough she ran away, and sold flowers on her own account, sharing a garret in

Whitechapel with three other girls, two of them
match-box makers, and the third a hawker like
herself. It was a hard life; but they got along
somehow, till she fell ill of a fever, and they took
her to the infirmary attached to the workhouse.
When she recovered they turned her out; and instead of going back to her garret she set out to
walk to Dover, where she hoped to find a young
man who had kept company with her, and who
had 'listed, and gone with his regiment to that
place.

Lord Ingleshaw made particular inquiries as to
her relations with this young man. He had been
employed at a horse-dealer's in Whitechapel. He
was an honest lad; had never got into trouble, so
far as she knew. He wanted to marry her as soon
as he had saved a little money, but in the mean
while he quarrelled with his master, and enlisted
in a cavalry regiment. The girl answered his lordship's questions without flinching. He could see
no sign of guilt in her manner. The story of her
youth and bringing up was wretched, but as common as it was wretched. She declared that she
had never been in prison; she had managed to
exist by honest labour, such as it was.

She had no knowledge of any other name than
Bess. The old woman had called her by that

name. Her young man had called her Starlight Bess, after a character in a play.

"We will give you a surname at once," said the Earl. "My daughter found you on a May morning. Suppose we call you Elizabeth May? I shall allow you to remain at the Castle in Tompion's charge for the present; and I hope you will take pains to learn all she can teach you. By and by I will see what can be done to place you in the way of earning your living. You must forget all about the young man at Dover. He is a soldier, and will have to go wherever his regiment may be ordered. You had better tell me his name, by the bye."

"Tom Brook."

The Earl wrote the name in his pocket-book.

"And you must promise me that you will hold no communication with him while you are in this house."

"I can't write," said the girl simply.

"Very good. But you must understand that you are not to communicate with Mr. Brook by any other means. And now you can go."

The girl, no longer Bess, but Elizabeth May, lifted her soft eyes gratefully to the Earl's face, made him a curtsy, and retired.

"She is the prettiest creature I ever saw,"

mused his lordship; "and she has the air of a lady, in spite of her vile English. This must be some waif from the superior classes that has drifted into the gutter."

———

CHAPTER IV.

OVER SUMMER SEAS.

"And ever as we sailed, our minds were full
    Of love and wisdom, which would overflow
In converse wild, and sweet, and wonderful;
    And in quick smiles whose light would come and go,
    Like music o'er wide waves."

MIDSUMMER-DAY had come and gone, and June was nearly over, before Lady Lucille was so far convalescent as to sit in an armchair by the open window of her dressing-room, and take afternoon tea with her father. The fever had been worse than Mr. Wharton apprehended. A famous physician had been down from London four times, merely to approve Mr. Wharton's treatment. Nurses and doctor had watched with unwavering care; and now the peril was past and gone, and Lady Lucille, pale, wan, and ethereal, reclined luxuriously in a nest of downy pillows, and sipped her tea, while her father watched her with eyes that were dimmed by happy tears. There had been a time—one terrible never-to-be-forgotten night—when he feared to lose this one jewel of his home.

Lady Lucille had had three nurses instead of two. Elizabeth May had pleaded with the doctor to be admitted to the sickroom, as a mere drudge to wait upon the trained nurses; and she had proved herself a genius at nursing.

"I believe she has a genius for everything," said Lucille, looking up at the girl who stood beside her chair, ready to take the cup and saucer which were almost too heavy a burden for the weak wasted hands. "Now that I am so much better, we can go on with our reading-lessons, Elizabeth."

"I shall be so glad of that, Lady Lucille. I have been learning with Tompion every day; and I've read to myself at night when I've been wakeful; and I think I've got on. But it will be so much nicer to learn with you."

"She has left off using vulgar expressions," said Lord Ingleshaw approvingly. "She reads her Bible daily, and she has been to church with Tompion. I think she is getting clearer ideas of what Christianity means."

Elizabeth looked at him gratefully with those gazelle eyes of hers. He, too, like Bruno Challoner, was one of the demi-gods, judged by that standard of humanity which was alone familiar to her. She looked with reverent admiration at the straight clearly-cut features, the thick gray hair brushed smoothly back from the broad open brow, the commanding gaze of the gray eyes, under strongly marked brows, darker than the hair. Among all her companions of the past there had been no such face as this.

Bruno Challoner was in London. Lord Ingleshaw, seeing that he was fretting himself into a fever, had insisted upon his leaving the Castle directly Lucille was pronounced out of danger.

"I'll send you half a dozen telegrams a day, if you like," said his lordship; "but I won't have you hanging about the corridors to question the nurses, or pacing the terrace, under Lucille's windows, half the night."

During the first fortnight of his betrothed's illness, Bruno had been in frequent communication with Elizabeth, who was, indeed, his chief informant about his darling's condition. She seemed more sympathetic than the hired nurses. She brought him messages from his love, and carried back his own loving messages and the flowers which he had gathered to adorn his darling's room. She was full of intelligence, divining his every thought, as it seemed to Bruno, with that wonderful keenness bred of stern necessity. Her devotion to the young lady, whose charity had opened the gates of a new world for her, was obvious in all her conduct.

"I believe that for once in my life I have met with the black swan, gratitude," Bruno told himself.

And now Bruno was getting rid of his life, as best he might, an exile from Ingleshaw. He slept at the house in Grosvenor-square, dined at his club, spent his days in masculine society, talked politics with incipient Cabinet Ministers flushed with the small triumphs of their first session, and planned his own entrance into public life. He had no heart for the amusements of London while Lucille was still an invalid. His spirits rose and fell in unison with the telegrams from the Castle. He would accept no invitation, and go to neither opera nor theatre. His only evening resort was the Strangers' Gallery in the House of Commons, where he combined instruction with amusement. Never did three weeks of his life hang more heavily on his hands.

She, who little more than a month ago had been Wild Bess, Black-eyed Bess, of Whitechapel, but who now answered meekly to the name of Elizabeth, had ample occupation for her mind during this glowing summer-tide. Her introduction to Ingleshaw Castle had been like a new birth. Pygmalion's animated statue could hardly have begun life more newly than this girl, suddenly transferred from the slums to the palace. Her eyes shone wide with wonder at a world where all things, animate and inanimate, were strange and beautiful. She had an intense appreciation of the Beautiful which surprised Lucille, who had been taught by the severely Aristotelian Marjorum that taste was the product of education, and was not to be expected from the ignorant.

Even Miss Marjorum was forced to admit that Elizabeth May showed a wonderful quickness at acquiring knowledge; but while owning as much as this, Lucille's governess in nowise sank her prejudice against her pupil's *protégée*. She would have disliked Elizabeth less had she been dull and slow. There was, to her mind, something uncanny, something impish, in this excessive quickness, this marvellous adaptability. That a creature plucked out of the quagmire of destitute dissolute East-end London could acquire all at once the graciousness of a lady, the low and musical tones of voice, the quiet measured movements, the tranquil beauty of educated girlhood—ay, of girlhood taught and trained through the slow course of years by Miss Marjorum—was a miracle that troubled and vexed the governess exceedingly. Of course this refinement was all surface—mere acting at best—a remarkable instance of mimetic power in the lower classes. Unfortunately, the Earl and his daughter were too ready to be deceived by these mimic graces. Already this characterless creditless damsel was accepted as a member of the Ingleshaw household, and sat at meat with the upper servants, or was served apart in her own bower—she who should have been proud to eat with kitchen-maids and footmen. There was no more talk of apprenticing her, or finding her service elsewhere. She was to learn the duties of an abigail from Tompion, and on Tompion's marriage with the under-butler—an event which had been impending for the last five years—Elizabeth May was to take Tompion's place. In the mean time there were small and gracious duties allotted to her. She dusted the books and china in Lady Lucille's rooms; she arranged the flowers, handling with light and delicate touch those exquisite exotics which were to her verily the revelation of unknown worlds. Lucille often made these flowers the text for a brief lecture on the countries from which they came, Elizabeth listening delightedly to the description of those far-away tropical regions.

During those quiet days of Lucille's convalescence, the girl whom she had rescued from ignorance and destitution was almost always in her company. It

was in vain that Miss Marjorum prophesied dismally
upon the evil consequences of this familiarity. The
girl behaved so well that it was difficult to object
to her presence. She was so eager to learn, that it
would have seemed in the last degree illiberal to
withhold knowledge. And it was the higher order
of knowledge for which this virgin mind thirsted.
When Lucille read passages of Milton or Shakespeare, Elizabeth listened enthralled. That story
of Hamlet—that passionate tragedy of Romeo and
Juliet—how deep was the magic of these to the
listener, whose imagination, for the first time, beheld that awful picture of Hamlet and the Ghost,
or glowed with delight at the image of Juliet bending from her balcony to whisper to her lover in the
sweet silence of the Italian midnight! To be eighteen, intelligent, of an impassioned temperament,
and to hear those stories for the first time! What
could surpass that rapture? To hear them, seated
in an Italian garden, steeped in the perfume of
countless roses, warmed to the very heart's core by
the sunshine of July! And a few weeks ago this
girl had lived in a loathsome alley, polluted with
unspeakable foulness, clamorous with rough riot
and vilest speech.

Against these Skakesperean studies, this introduction of the gutter-bred girl to the sublimest

heights of imaginative literature, Miss Marjorum protested vehemently.

"What do you mean to make of her?" she asked. "Don't you see that you are spoiling her for domestic service by trying to give her these elevated tastes?"

"I am not trying," answered Lucille. "Elevated taste is as natural to her as his song is to the thrush. Can't you see that God created her full of imagination and cleverness, and that she has only been waiting the opportunity of development? She need not spend her life in domestic service. She takes so kindly to education that I shall teach her all I can; and I know you will help me, dear Marjy, and by and by we shall find plenty of use for her intelligence. If you will only take her in hand, she may some day earn her living by teaching others, as honourably as you have done for the last twenty years."

This argument was unanswerable, and the softened Marjorum replied gently,

"You forget, my dear, that it is not every one who has the teacher's capacity. The power to impart information is a peculiar gift. This girl may be quick in picking up ideas, in a superficial sort of way; but I doubt if she possesses any of the solid qualities which go to make a competent instructress of youth."

"Only try your hand upon her, Marjy dear. I'm sure you could make something out of a black girl from Otaheite."

Marjorum, thus flattered and caressed into compliance by the pupil whom she fondly loved, and in whose married home she hoped by and by to make her nest, allowed her prejudices to be lulled to sleep. She took Elizabeth in hand, and put her through a severe educational process for a space of three hours daily; and once having put her hand to the plough, Miss Marjorum drove her furrow vigorously. She was glad to have an occasion for the bringing forth of that educational machinery which Lucille had outgrown and done with. The equator, Lindley Murray, latitude and longitude, the sidereal heavens, the earth's formation, the animal, vegetable, and mineral kingdoms, were all brought into play. Elizabeth laboured and learned obediently, indefatigably. It was dryasdust work; but her benefactress wished her so to learn; and she never faltered, any more than she had faltered when Tompion introduced her to the feminine art of needlework by making her sew interminable seams in the stiffest calico.

When her morning studies were over Elizabeth

had her reward in an afternoon and evening given
to music, art, and poetry. Her mind grew and
widened under this double tuition. The knowledge
of dry hard facts helped her to a higher appreciation of poetry. Never, perhaps, did education pro-
ceed so quickly.

And now Lucille was so far recovered that the
doctor declared she needed only a change to sea
air to become as strong and well as she had been
before that fatal May morning; so Miss Marjorum
was despatched to Weymouth, attended by the
under-butler, to find a furnished house facing the
sea; and having selected one particular house, distinguishable only by its superior freshness and purity
of furniture and decoration, from a terrace of houses
all exactly alike, Miss Marjorum telegraphed the
accomplishment of her mission; whereupon Lord
Ingleshaw himself escorted his daughter to Weymouth, attended by Tompion and Elizabeth May,
who travelled together in a second-class carriage,
an opportunity which Tompion improved by various
remarks upon favourites, flatterers, and sycophants
in the abstract, and of the brief tenure of favour
usually enjoyed by such persons; all of which sen-
tentious utterances Miss May heard with the calm
smile of scorn, feeling herself as much superior to
Tompion as she knew herself inferior to Lady Lucille.

Lord Ingleshaw spent a few days with his daughter, who was now in such perfect health and spirits, that this change of air prescribed by the doctor seemed a mere formula. They drove about the shady rustic roads, sailed on the summer sea, explored the arid heights of Portland, drank of the Wishing-well, admired the White Horse, and thoroughly enjoyed life in this calm restful fashion. And then Lord Ingleshaw departed on a visit to a friend in the North, where there was to be great slaughter of grouse a little later on.

"I daresay Bruno will be running down to have a peep at you," he said on the morning he left Weymouth. "I have given him permission to come."

Lucille blushed and sparkled, and kissed her father by way of answer. She had been longing to see her lover for the last month. He had written to her daily, but she had been forbidden to answer his letters, which seemed a hard thing. He had sent her books, music, trifles of every kind calculated to beguile the tedium of illness, and she had only been allowed to thank him through that stately medium, Miss Marjorum. She had not been allowed to look at the letter which conveyed her gratitude, lest scarlet fever should be transmitted by a look.

And now he was coming, he was coming! She could have shouted for joy. Tremulous with hope

and gladness, she stood on the balcony overhanging
the bright picturesque bay, and looked along the
parade for that gracious fly which should convey
Mr. Challoner and his portmanteau from the station.
The Italian band was playing *Don Giovanni* below
her windows—melodies brimming over with joyous
love, like that which filled her soul.

"Surely, my dear Lucille, you are going for a
walk or a drive this delightful morning!" said Miss
Marjorum, coming in from the back drawing-room,
where Elizabeth sat meekly writing out a page of
grammatical analysis, with the laborious slowness
of one to whom penmanship and grammar were
new arts.

"No, Marjy dearest, not to-day. I am watching
for Bruno," answered Lucille from the balcony.

"Deh, vieni alla finestra," played the band below, while the happy bathers splashed and bounded
in the blue water beyond that crescent of yellow
sand.

"But, my dear Lucille, you have no justification
for expecting him this morning, or even to-day,"
expostulated Miss Marjorum. "His lordship merely
stated, as a general fact, that Mr. Challoner was
now at liberty to pay you a visit."

"And do you think he will not come directly he
is free?" exclaimed Lucille. "Would I not go to

him—like an arrow from a bow—if I were told I might go? I expect him this instant."

"You will, at least, allow that he can hardly come, until the train brings him, and there is none due till half-past three."

"How horribly matter-of-fact you are!" cried Lucille. "No, I suppose he would come by train. Post-horses would be slower, and balloons are so erratic. Please give me the time-table."

She ran rapidly over that bewildering document.

"No, I can't make out anything. My brain is in a whirl. The trains seem to go everywhere except to this place. Yes, here is the column at last. Weymouth—Weymouth! No; not till half-past three. How horrible!"

"Had you not better go for a nice country drive?" suggested Miss Marjorum. "It would divert your mind."

"Nothing less than an earthquake would divert my mind," retorted Lucille impatiently. "I don't believe in your time-table. I'll go and sit on the beach, if you like; but I shall be expecting Bruno every instant. Has Elizabeth finished her lessons?"

Miss Marjorum inspected the page of analysis in the stiff newly-acquired round-hand, looking down at the exercise majestically over Elizabeth's shoulder.

"Yes, she has just finished."

"Then she can come with me," said Lucille, putting on her hat and gloves, and taking up a volume of Shakespeare. "Bring your work, Lizzie, and come and sit on the beach."

Elizabeth ran off to put on her hat, and returned in two minutes, the image of propriety, in her neat-fitting black cashmere gown, linen collar, and small black straw hat. She carried a basket containing an antimacassar, for she had already advanced from endless calico seams to high-art needlework.

The two girls tripped lightly down to the beach, away from the bathers and the children, to a spot that was almost secluded, though the confined limits of the bay do not give much opportunity for seclusion. They found an empty boat which helped to screen them from the rest of the world, and, seated in its shadow, Lucille opened her Shakespeare.

"I am going to read to you, Lizzie. Shall it be *Romeo and Juliet?*"

"Whatever you like, Lady Lucille."

Lucille began at the ballroom scene, the dawn of Juliet's love, and went on, skipping a scene here and there, to the balcony scene. She had nearly finished this when there came a step upon the loose pebbles of the beach, and she dropped the book suddenly, and rose to her feet.

Yes, it was Bruno! She would have known his step among a thousand. Another moment, and she was clasped to his breast, still sheltered by that friendly boat, while Elizabeth walked away discreetly, leaving the lovers to themselves for a little while. There is a universal etiquette in these things, founded upon the universality of human nature, which prevails from Mayfair to Whitechapel.

"My darling, how more than happy I am to be with you!" exclaimed Bruno. "I never thought that I should live to consider it my greatest misfortune not to have had scarlet fever. My own one, do not think that it was my vile cowardice which parted us all this time. I had no fear of the fever. I would have watched by your pillow day and night, if I had been allowed. But I could not rebel against your father. I best proved my love of his daughter by obedience to him."

"I know, Bruno. I have never doubted your unselfishness or your love. But it has been a long parting. I did not think it possible days and hours could seem so long," said Lucille naïvely.

"Be assured they have not seemed longer to you than they have been to me, love. And now let us sit side by side, and you shall tell me all you have to tell. Thank God you are well again—the very image of blooming health—and lovelier than ever!"

"But how did you get here, Bruno? Marjy and I examined the time-table; there was no train due till half-past three."

"Perhaps you only looked at one time-table. I came by the Great Western."

"What, are there two railways? How sweet of the Great Western to bring you ever so much sooner than I hoped!"

And then they gave themselves up to lovers' talk, which must seem mere drivel, sheer imbecility, if set down formally in black and white, but full of deepest tenderest meaning for these two. They sat under the hull of the big lubberly fishing-boat, and told each other all they had thought, and felt, and suffered during the weary time of severance.

Elizabeth strolled upon the beach a little way off, within call, should she be wanted. She looked back now and then at those two figures under the boat, but they gave no indication of wanting her, though she had been strolling up and down that stretch of sand and pebble for one slow sunny hour. For the first time since she had been at Weymouth she felt inexpressibly lonely; for the first time since she had seen the place the beauty of that southern bay, shut in from the outer world by green headlands on one side and by Portland's bold peninsula on the other, began to pall upon her. In a moment, as it were, her soul grew weary of blue sea and yellow sands, summer sky, undulating green hills, and all the glory and freshness of the summer day. What was it all to her, or to any lonely uncared-for creature, more than a picture on a wall—a thing in which she had no part?

"Better to be in Ramshackle-court, where I had plenty of people of my own kind to talk to," she thought sullenly, when the second hour had begun, and the lovers still sat, absorbed, their heads bent towards each other, like flowers inclining on their stems. An hour ago she had been Lucille's companion, and life had seemed full of interest. Now she was Lucille's servant, a being quite remote from the young lady's existence.

Nature had given this child of the gutter warm feelings—some good, some bad. Among the latter was jealousy, of which she had more than the common share. She almost hated Bruno for having banished her from Lady Lucille's company. Yes, even Bruno, that demi-god, whose voice had tones which moved her almost to tears—whose eyes had glances that made her shrink and tremble.

Better to be among her own people, amidst filth and squalor, evil ways and evil language? No, that was a lunatic's impulse. Could she, who had escaped from that pandemonium into the paradise of refinement and clean living, calmly contemplate the being flung back into that gulf of horror? No; a thousand times no. And yet, without sympathy, without the company of some one she loved and admired, the placid luxury of her present life was hateful to her. She had grown fastidious in this new atmosphere. Food and raiment, air and sunshine, comfort and shelter, were no longer all-sufficient for her. Heretofore in a life of perpetual want and difficulty the cravings of physical nature had been paramount. Now the spiritual nature predominated. The sharper pangs of heart-hunger had begun.

At last, when she had grown as weary of that smiling summer scene as ever she had felt of those wet windy streets, along which she had toiled, drabbled and muddy, with her basket of sickly flowers, in the days of her slavery, Lucille and her lover rose and walked slowly across the sands towards that lonely figure.

"We are going home, Elizabeth," said the lady. "It must be nearly time for luncheon."

"Nearly!" exclaimed Bess. "It is half-past two. I heard the clock strike ever so long ago."

"Poor thing, why did you wait for me? I daresay you have been longing to go to your dinner," said Lucille compassionately.

"I don't care a straw about dinner," answered Bess contemptuously; "only—only I don't like to be left and forgotten—as if—as if I was an umbrella."

The delicate face flushed deepest carnation, and the large dark eyes sparkled with an angry fire, as the girl spoke. Bruno burst out laughing, moved by the absurdity of this outbreak of temper in a brand snatched from the burning.

"I am sorry I forgot you," said Lucille gently, but with a gravity which reminded Bess of the gulf between them. "Mr. Challoner and I are going to luncheon. Take the books and the basket, please, and make haste back to your dinner."

Lucille and her lover walked slowly towards the parade, leaving Bess to gather up the books and work-basket from under the lee of the boat.

"A decided exhibition of the cloven foot," said Bruno, smiling. "I begin to think you've caught a Tartar, Lucille."

"She was never impertinent or ill-tempered before. I don't understand it in the least."

"I'm afraid I do. You've heard the vulgar proverb about setting a beggar on horseback. You have been rather too indulgent with that young person, and she is beginning to give herself airs. May I inquire what is the position which she occupies in your household? Is she your companion, or your maid?"

"She will be my maid by and by, when Tompion marries; and, in the mean time, Marjy and I are trying to educate her. She is so quick and intelligent that it is a pleasure to teach her."

"Is there not a fear that you may make her too clever for her place? Tompion never struck me as an intellectual prodigy."

"Poor Tompion! she is very dull."

"Exactly, but an efficient servant."

"An excellent servant," admitted Lucille.

"Which I fear this young person will never become under your present process. My darling, your sweetness is spoiling her. You have made her insolent already; and the next thing will be the necessity of her dismissal."

"No, no, Bruno; you do not know what a beautiful nature she has. I cannot tell you how devoted she was to me while I was ill—what an untiring nurse, what an affectionate companion."

"I know she was deeply anxious about you, as she had good reason to be. I saw her very often in those sad days at Ingleshaw. She was the only person who ever gave me detailed information about my darling."

"And she used to bring me flowers and messages from you. Sometimes when my mind was all astray, and it was difficult for me to understand what people said to me, she would take pains to let me know that you were near and sorry for me. Do you want me to forget all that, Bruno, now that I am well and that you are with me?"

"No, dear, but I want you to be reasonable. A girl picked out of the gutter is a rough diamond at best. Such a gem must require a great deal of polishing before it is worthy to shine side by side with my pearl of price."

All Lucille's thoughts on that day of reunion were given to her lover. They lunched together. Miss Marjorum—very sharp set after the unaccustomed delay—counting for no more than if she had been a painter's lay-figure. They went for a long ramble together after luncheon, Lucille being eager to make Bruno acquainted with the rural beauties of the surrounding scenery. The landscape around Weymouth is not particularly poetic or striking; but it is rustic and pretty, fertile, varied by hill and hollow, with more timber than is usually to be found in the region of the sea. Bruno thought those country lanes, those grassy hills, the realisation of paradise. The lovers walked and talked, and talked and walked, forgetting time and distance, mankind and the world, until they had need to hasten in order to reach the house on the parade in time for the eight-o'clock dinner.

"I am afraid you must be dreadfully tired," said Bruno, as they neared the town; "I ought not to have let you walk so far."

"I don't feel as if I had walked a mile," answered Lucille; "I never felt stronger or better in my life."

Tompion was waiting to dress her young mistress, and during that hurried toilet Lucille had no time to make any inquiry about Elizabeth, nor was Tompion disposed to volunteer information. She had been standing on her dignity ever since Elizabeth's appearance in the household.

Bruno and his betrothed spent the evening absorbed in each other and Mozart, while Miss Marjorum slumbered placidly in the twilight of the back drawing-room, feeling that she was fulfilling all her duties as a dragon of prudery by the mere fact of her presence. Her slumbering figure, the very image of middle-aged repose, was also the incarnation of the proprieties.

The next morning was gray and showery; but Bruno, too happy to sleep late o' mornings, had left his hotel for an early swim before the blinds were drawn up at the house on the parade. When he had had his swim he went for a walk on the sands, careless of light showers. Sea and sky were a dull gray, with gleams of watery light touching the waves here and there.

He had walked some distance, and was nearing the point of the bay, when he overtook a solitary young woman in black. He recognised the tall slim figure, the graceful walk, that free untutored grace which comes of an active life.

"Good-morning, Elizabeth," he said, overtaking her; "you are out very early."

She started at the sound of his voice, and turned to meet him, with the same vivid carnation which he had noted yesterday—a blush that might mean surprise, anger, shyness, anything, but which heightened her beauty.

"Why shouldn't I be out?" she asked. "I suppose the sands are as free to me as to you, though I am a servant."

This was an impulse of her old unregenerate nature, which prompted her to defiance of her superiors as a kind of self-defence.

"All the world is free to youth and intellect," said Bruno coolly. "Why are you so disagreeable? I thought you were a good-tempered, well-meaning young woman, when I saw you at Ingleshaw."

"I hope I shall always mean well to those who are good to me," answered the girl; "but I don't

like to be taken up like a plaything, and cast aside
and forgotten."

"How do you mean?"

"Till you came I was with Lady Lucille almost
every hour of the day. She taught me, she read to
me, she let me sit by her when she played the
piano; I got to know all her favourite tunes. But
when you came she left me on the beach and forgot me. I have not seen her or heard her voice
since then. All yesterday afternoon and evening I
sat alone in my little room at the top of the house,
and watched the sea."

"Why prefer solitude when there were Tompion
and Mrs. Prince in the housekeeper's room? You
might have been with them."

"No, I mightn't. I hate them and they hate
me. I have been a flower-girl; but I am not a
servant, and I can't get on with servants."

"Then I'm afraid you'll have to leave Ingleshaw
Castle. You can hardly expect to spend your life
in the drawing-room with an Earl's daughter."

"Lady Lucille said she was fond of me, and
that she wanted to teach me to be a lady. Why
cannot I be with her, if she likes to have me?"

"Because you are a foolish and ungrateful young
woman," replied Bruno, hardening his heart against
this girl, whose lovely eyes were fixed upon his

face with an appealing look which was full of pathos. "You are not content to enjoy Lady Lucille's society when it is convenient to her to have you with her. You give yourself offended airs because she prefers her future husband to a person whom she has known only two months, and of whose character and belongings she knows nothing."

"When I love people I love them with all my soul; I love them until love is like a pain—a slow gnawing pain that eats my heart," answered the girl impetuously. "What difference does it make to me that Lady Lucille is an Earl's daughter? She and I are made of the same flesh and blood, are we not?"

"No doubt; but eighteen years' culture and training are in themselves a distinction, to say nothing of hereditary influences," said Bruno, answering his own thoughts rather than that passionate speaker.

He had been wondering at the delicate beauty, the grand carriage of this gutter-bred creature; the daring with which she asserted herself, and claimed indulgence for her passionate feelings—she who belonged to the class which has been taught from its cradle to cringe and whine.

And then gravely yet kindly he took her to task for her folly.

"My good girl," he said, "you are altogether
wrong in your manner of looking at your new life.
Lady Lucille has been very kind to you—kinder
than one young lady in twenty would have been;
so kind that she has run counter to the opinion of
her father, her governess, and myself, in order to
gratify her inclination to help you. But this goodness of hers can give you no claim upon her, beyond
the common claim of your helplessness. You have
no right to exact more than it is wise or convenient
for her to give. If you are willing to be a true
and faithful servant to her, to respect her position
and your own place as a servant, there is no reason
she should not please herself by keeping you in
her service; but if you are subject to jealous tempers,
she had better find you a place elsewhere, where
your affection for your mistress will be less intense, and your notions of a servant's duty will be
clearer."

Elizabeth's heart beat loud and fast as she
listened to his cold and measured words. Was it
hatred of the speaker which made her so angry?
Her passionate soul revolted at the idea of these
differences of rank, which made it an impertinence
in her to love her benefactress with a jealous and
exacting love. Ever since she had been able to
think she had been a Radical. Her daring intellect

had overleapt the barriers of rank and fortune. Tramping in the mud—bonnetless, almost shoeless —she had looked at the women in carriages, and had told herself that she was as good as they. To her, as to the rugged philosopher Carlyle, it had seemed that the difference between beauty in the gutter and beauty in a three-hundred-guinea barouche was only a question of clothes. She had never heard of hereditary influences—the slow and gradual development of privileged races, the perpetual imperceptible education of favourable surroundings.

"If I was to be no better than a servant—a dog to fetch and to carry, and to eat and drink and get fat—why did Lady Lucille teach me, and read to me, and let me hear her play?" asked Bess. "She never did as much as that for Tompion."

"And she was very foolish when she did it for you. She has spoiled the makings of a good servant."

"I'll try to prove you wrong in that," answered Bess, frowning defiance at him. "If I am to be a servant, I'll be a good one. I'll show you that I can keep my place as well as any of them."

"I shall be very glad to find you can do so,"

replied Bruno, turning upon his heel, and leaving the damsel to her reflections.

It was not without compunction that he so left her. He would have liked to have said something kind at parting; but she had shown him the danger of over-much kindness. She was evidently a person who must be ruled with a high hand.

He breakfasted with Lady Lucille and Miss Marjorum, and left them almost immediately after breakfast. He had some business to transact at the other end of the town, he told Lucille—a fact which she was inwardly inclined to resent. What business had he to be anywhere except with her?

When he was gone, Miss Marjorum summoned Elizabeth to her morning studies in the back drawing-room. The girl came, the image of meek obedience, but with pallid cheeks, and red rings round her eyes.

"You have been crying," said Miss Marjorum severely.

"I had the toothache," faltered Bess, with her swollen eyelids drooping over the dark eyes.

"And you cried because of the toothache? What childish want of self-command! Are you aware of the great mass of suffering that is always going on in this world; and can you shed tears for any petty pain of your own?"

"One's own pains hurt most," answered Bess. "I daresay other people cry about theirs."

"Only people who are without fortitude and submission to the will of God," answered Miss Marjorum. "All suffering is sent us for our benefit."

"Then I had rather not be benefited—in that way," said Bess, so meekly that her instructress could hardly resent the remark.

Then came the usual morning's work—multiplication-tables, weights and measures, English grammar, a little geography, a little English history—just that elementary knowledge which would bring Elizabeth May on a level with the lowest form in a Board school. But dryasdust as the lessons were, Elizabeth gave all the powers of her mind to the comprehension and digestion of them. She learnt with a quickness that astonished her teacher, who had never before taught any one with whom lessons meant rescue from the dismal swamp of ignorance and vulgarity.

Elizabeth was still bending over her page of parsing when Bruno came in, flushed and joyous-looking, smelling of sea-breezes and sunshine.

"Lucille, I want you to come for a cruise in my yacht," he said.

"Your yacht!" exclaimed Lucille, starting up from her work, delighted at her lover's return.

"That is a tremendous joke! How should you come by a yacht?"

"In the most sordid and commonplace manner—I have hired one."

"Then that was your business this morning?"

"Precisely."

"O you darling! Pray forgive me."

"For what?"

"For my wickedness. I thought it was so unkind of you to have business at the other end of the town when I wanted you here."

"My business was to charter a vessel in which we can explore the coast between Bournemouth and Dawlish. You behold the skipper of the Urania sloop, forty tons, crew five men and a boy. For one month certain I· am her proud proprietor."

"And you know how to yacht?" inquired Lucille naïvely.

"I had some small experience in that line in the Mediterranean; but I have engaged the captain of the Urania—an old salt. You needn't be afraid to trust yourself on my boat."

"I would sail across the Atlantic with you in a cockle-shell," said Lucille.

They were standing on the balcony, out of everybody's hearing, and could afford to be foolish.

"We should both go to the bottom," answered

Bruno; "but it would be happiness. There she is! How do you like her? Lovely, isn't she?" he asked, gazing seaward.

"I did not know you had any friends here," said Lucille, looking along the parade with a by no means rapturous expression. She thought her lover had been talking of some fair promenader.

"No more I have, sweet, nor hardly a feminine friend in this wide world except you. The Urania, love, yonder against the blue. I sent her round that you might look at her. Are not her lines graceful?"

"She looks very pretty, and how coquettishly she bobs to the sea!" said Lucille, as the Urania dipped her nose to the water. "When am I to go on board her?"

"Directly after luncheon, if you like. We might come home to a nine-o'clock dinner."

"Never mind luncheon. Let us pack up some biscuits and things, and go at once," exclaimed Lucille, with her eyes on the sloop. "She doesn't take the slightest notice of us. Have you any means of communicating with the captain?"

"Only a handkerchief. I told him to keep his eye on these houses," answered Bruno, waving his white silk handkerchief. "Now he will lay to, and

send a boat on shore, and you and Miss Marjorum
can come as soon as you please."

Lucille ran to the back drawing-room to tell
the governess what bliss awaited her.

"We are going at once—at once," she exclaimed, after she had rapidly related Bruno's ac-
quisition of the Urania. "Put on your mushroom-
hat directly, like a darling, and bring your biggest
sunshade. You can come, Elizabeth. Run down
and tell Prince to pack a basket of luncheon, with
everything nice that she can get in five minutes—
wine, too, for Mr. Challoner, and lemonade for us.
And you can bring some nice books with you,
though I don't suppose any one will want to read;
and my crewel-basket, though I'm sure I sha'n't
work."

Lucille was gone before Miss Marjorum could
question or remonstrate. There was nothing to be
done but obey. If she declined to go, the lovers
would assuredly go without her; and though the
proprieties, as observed between engaged people,
might be stretched to allow of a country walk, they
would be seriously outraged by yachting without a
chaperon. Miss Marjorum loved not the sea, nor
the sea her. At her best, she could just manage
to escape sea-sickness by maintaining a statuesque
immobility which hardly permitted her to think.

She would have liked to do her voyages under the influence of chloroform, were that possible.

All the gray clouds had drifted away; the sky was one unbroken blue. Poor Miss Marjorum could not hint a doubt of the weather. She went up to her room, and put on her brown mushroom-hat, and was ready to start when Mrs. Prince's basket was packed—a task which took so long as to make Lucille impatient.

At last everything was ready, and in less than a quarter of an hour afterwards they were all on board—Miss Marjorum seated in a luxurious nest of cushions and shawls, outwardly the image of repose, but inwardly suffering, a *Quarterly Review* lying open in her lap, at an interesting paper on Herder, of which she was incapable of reading a line; Lucille dancing about the deck after Bruno, looking at this and that, and asking innumerable questions; Elizabeth May sitting in a corner apart, the very furthest corner available, working diligently, and never lifting her eyes from her work.

She had been told that she ought to remember her position as a servant, and she wanted to show Bruno Challoner that she did so remember herself.

They went coasting around by picturesque cliffs; they saw caves, and other wonders of the shore— jelly-fish, and other marvels of the deep. Life, for

two out of these four, was steeped in the sunshine
that lights an earthly paradise. The summer sea,
the summer air, were full of rapture. The other
two sat still and silently endured—one the agony
of suppressed sea-sickness, the other suppressed
heartache; though why her heart should ache
Elizabeth May hardly knew.

"Why should the sight of their happiness make
me miserable?" she asked herself. "Am I made
up of envy and jealousy?"

Many days came after this—long summer days
of peerless weather, fresh seas, and flowing sails.
They spent every day on the Urania. Miss Marjorum's silent sufferings grew less acute. Custom
dulled the edge of agony; or it may be that, in the
language of the captain, Miss Marjorum was getting
her sea-legs. Elizabeth went with them every day,
always provided with her work-basket, but she
worked very little now, and no longer sat in a remote corner. Were she ever so willing to keep
her place as a servant, it was not easy for her to
do so, when Lucille was inclined to treat her as a
companion; and Lucille was so inclined always
most especially on board the yacht, where the innocent happiness of Bruno's betrothed overflowed
in kindliness to everybody. She had the sweetest
words and looks even for the sunburnt weather-

beaten old sailors. She made much of them, and gave them dainties out of her ample picnic-basket, and spoiled them for future service, giving them false views of young ladyhood.

Bruno hired a funny little piano, built on purpose for a yacht, and to this he and his betrothed sang many a lover's duet on calm evenings. By and by Lucille discovered that Elizabeth had a fine contralto voice, whereupon she taught the girl to take part in the "Canadian Boat-Song," "Blow, Gentle Gales," and other sea-going glees. Bruno felt that it was foolish, wrong even, to make this girl the companion of their lives, she whose earlier life was unknown to them, save by her unattested record of bare facts. He remonstrated with Lucille, and then gave way. It was true that Elizabeth was an exceptional person; the lowness of her bringing up had left no indelible stamp of vulgarity. She grew more refined in manner and diction, nay, even in ideas, every day of her life. It was impossible to dispute her innate superiority; a rough diamond perhaps, but assuredly a diamond of purest water, and one that took kindly to the polishing process.

She had never lost her temper since that first day. If the lovers forgot or neglected her, she sat apart and held her peace, patiently awaiting Lucille's pleasure; or she sat at Miss Marjorum's feet and read aloud, her instructress feeling very proud of her progress.

For nearly six weeks they lived this happy life. Lord Ingleshaw sometimes joined them for a few days; and on those occasions Elizabeth May fell into the background of their existence, keeping respectfully aloof from the grave gray-bearded elderly man, whom she regarded with deepest awe. They explored every bit of the coast, from Durlstone Head to the Start Point, sometimes spending a couple of nights on board the Urania, until Miss Marjorum grew so familiar with Neptune, that it was a wonder to her to think she had ever been a bad sailor.

In all these summer days of varying weather Elizabeth never wearied of the sea, whether she sat alone and apart, absorbed in her own thoughts, or joined in the amusements of Lady Lucille and Mr. Challoner. The sea was a source of unfailing delight to her. It was the wildest grandest thing she had ever seen. Mountain and moorland she knew not, nor prairie, nor forest; the green fields and low hills of Kent were all she had seen of Nature's grandeur, until she came suddenly face to face with ocean. Her first experience of a tempest was rapture. She stood on deck, lashed and beaten by the rain, buffeted by the wind, and watched the lightning gleaming on the dark leaden waters, and the livid white crests of the waves that seemed to leap up against the blackened sky, and gloried in the tumult of the scene. She loved the calm summer aspect of the sea all the more intensely after she had seen the might and horror of the storm.

The happiest days must end. September was nearly over. The days were shortening, the evening breezes were growing chill, albeit the noontides were as sunny as midsummer. Bruno was to surrender his command of the Urania in a day or two; and Lucille and her governess were under orders for Ingleshaw Castle, where his lordship had already taken up his abode in readiness for the pheasant-shooting. There was to be no parting between these happy lovers; but their sea-going days were over; and Lucille's spirit was shadowed by a faint cloud of melancholy at the thought that such blissful days could come to an end.

"I wonder whether we shall ever come to Weymouth again?" she said, looking dreamily at the picturesque bay from her low luxurious seat on deck.

"I don't know, love; I think our next yachting experiences should be in more romantic waters—off the Orkneys or the Hebrides."

"I think I would rather come here again; we can never be happier than we have been here," said Lucille softly.

"Yes, yes, we can; our souls may take a higher flight in bolder grander scenes; we will sail under Italian skies, over the tideless blue of the Mediterranean. I will show you Capri, Paestum, Cyprus; there shall be a perpetual crescendo in our happiness!"

"That cannot be, Bruno; nothing can surpass perfection; and I have been perfectly happy here."

"You are too logical for me," he said, with a faint sigh.

"How wearily you spoke just then!" exclaimed Lucille, looking at him with sudden anxiety; "you have had such a pale and tired look for the last few days, Bruno. I hope you are not ill."

"Ill? no; I was never better in my life. But there is a certain tameness in this coast; it is just possible to get tired of it. I am glad we are going back to Ingleshaw."

"For the sake of shooting those poor pheasants. What a pity that even the most amiable Englishman should be created with a propensity to murder!"

This was their last day. They had gone for a long sail, and it was late in the evening when they neared Weymouth, under a full moon.

This day had not been so perfectly happy as other days. Bruno was tired, or out of spirits. Lucille could not tell which. He did not interest himself in the sailing of the yacht, never touching a rope all through the day, he who was usually so active. He lay on a rug at Lucille's feet, reading a newspaper or talking to her, in a somewhat listless fashion. And now, in the moonlight, he was pacing the little deck, with a restless air that seemed like a rebellion against the narrow space to which he was confined.

Lucille went down into the cabin to fetch an extra wrap, and stayed there for about a quarter of an hour talking to Miss Marjorum, who was comfortably esconced on the sofa, placidly digesting a very good dinner. On her return to the deck, Lucille saw Bruno and Elizabeth seated side by side, the girl's face clearly visible in the bright moonlight—a pale impassioned face turned towards Bruno, with tears streaming down the cheeks. He had his hand on her shoulder, and he was talking to her in a voice so low that it was drowned by the faint plash of the waves, yet with an unmistakable earnestness of manner.

For a few moments Lucille stood aghast. The passionate imploring look in the girl's eyes, the attitude of the man, which seemed one of appeal or

entreaty—what could these mean except that one
hideous treason which would change the colour of
Lucille Challoner's life? She stood as if changed
to stone; she felt as if she had suddenly stepped
upon the edge of an abyss, saw the black gulf
yawning below her, and knew that she must fall
into it. Only for a few moments did she stand
looking at those two figures in the bows, every line
clearly defined in the broad silver light, and then
she advanced towards them with a quiet step, and
looked at them with a frank and not unfriendly
gaze, slow to believe in evil, despite this agony of
doubt gnawing her heart.

"Is there anything the matter, Bruno?"

He had started ever so slightly at her footstep,
but he looked up at her now steadily enough, with
grave unabashed eyes, his hand still resting lightly
on Elizabeth's shoulder.

"Only the realisation of my own fear. This
girl is not happy in the artificial life she has been
leading with us. It does not suit her temper or
her temperament. You must find her more occupation, regular duties, a place to fill in your father's
household, or in somebody else's. This idle orna-
mental life of ours wearies her."

He rose from the bench, leaving Elizabeth sitting there, silent, downcast.

"Is this true, Elizabeth?" asked Lucille.

"Yes."

"Then you should have made your complaints to me and not to Mr. Challoner; he can hardly be expected to understand your feelings," Lucille answered, in colder accents than Bruno had ever heard before from her lips.

"What did she say to you, Bruno?" Lucille asked presently, when she and her lover were standing side by side, out of Elizabeth's hearing.

"O, I hardly know!" he answered, with a touch of impatience. "Another outburst of temper like that of which I told you six weeks ago. You have been most unwise in your treatment of her. Instead of being grateful, she is discontented with her position. I warned you against this result, Lucille."

"How harshly you speak, Bruno! I could not help being fond of the girl, and I did not think she could be ungrateful," said Lucille slowly.

She had hardly recovered from the bewilderment which had seized her at sight of those two figures—the pale face wet with tears, the passionate eyes turned towards Bruno. Her lover's explanation, given with such a cold matter-of-fact air, went far to satisfy her; but it was not altogether satisfactory. Unused as she was to encounter falsehood, unsuspicious as she was of wrong, she had yet an unhappy feeling, as of one who walks in the dark with a vague sense of danger close at hand. She could hardly see the lamp-lit semicircle of the bay, the white houses gleaming in the moonlight, for the tears that clouded her eyes, tears wrung from a nameless agony.

She hardly spoke to Bruno during the business of landing, and it was only when they were on the doorstep that Bruno found anything to say to her, and then it was but to bid a brief good-night. All their plans were made for the next day—Bruno was to meet them at the station and escort them to Ingleshaw.

CHAPTER V.

A LEAF FROM THE BOOK OF THE PAST.

"Sir, you and I must part,—but that's not it:
Sir, you and I have loved,—but there's not it."

IT was the first week in October, and the woods at Ingleshaw were deepening to that sombre green which precedes the glory of the autumnal reds and yellows; the chestnuts had already put on the tawny hue of decay, and the russet leaves fell heavily on the soft grass in the avenue; but oaks and beeches held their own yet against the destroyer.

The gardens were vivid with gaudy autumn flowers; but the roses still bloomed in sheltered places, and the hothouses were full of summer bloom.

Life at Ingleshaw Castle moved upon more conventional lines than that unceremonious existence on board the Urania. Lucille and her lover no longer spent their days in almost unbroken companionship, albeit they were living under one roof. Lord Ingleshaw was fond of shooting, and expected

Bruno to be equally enthusiastic; so these two spent most of their mornings in the woods, with a keeper and a couple of dogs, shooting pheasants in the old-fashioned country-squire or country-parson style.

Lucille's aunt, Lady Carlyon, had arrived at the Castle on a visit of indefinite duration.

"I shall stay as long as ever you contrive to keep me amused, my dear," she said; "so it will be your own fault if I go away soon. Ingleshaw is quite the dullest place I know; but there is a soothing influence in its dulness which always makes me feel better afterwards—like what people say of the Engadine, don't you know. It's not that you feel particularly well while you are there, but you find yourself in such splendid health directly you get away."

To amuse Lady Carlyon was no light duty. She liked her niece to go to her at half-past eight with her early cup of tea, and read little bits of the newspaper to her before she got up. This helped her brain to awake, she said. She required company in her morning saunter round the gardens. She wanted her niece's sympathy with her crewel-work, an art which she carried to great perfection, but for which she required a good deal of as-sistance from other people. She liked to have one of Mr. Anthony Trollope's novels read to her; and she entered warmly into the loves and perplexities of his young people. She liked to hear her favourite bits of Mozart. In fact, she liked to keep Lucille about her in an elegant kind of slavery all day long; while poor Lucille was longing to be trudging through the woods, following the far-off sound of the guns, so as to meet the sportsmen after their morning's work, and sit on some grassy bank with them while they ate their picnic luncheon.

Lady Carlyon professed herself delighted at her niece's engagement.

"I think I could hardly have done better for you myself, if I had brought you out next season," she said. "No doubt your father always intended you and Bruno to marry. It is such a comfortable way of adjusting things. Bruno will have the estate, and you will have a good deal of money, without which Bruno would have found it rather difficult to manage."

"Aunt Ethel, you surely don't think—" began Lucille, turning very pale.

"I don't think that he cares more for the money than for you!" cried the dowager; "of course I don't. What a silly sensitive child you are! Everybody knows that he adores you; but the money will be very useful to him, all the same. It

will make it much easier for him to be a good
landlord. Nobody ought to depend solely on land
nowadays. Your father tells me that you and
Bruno are to be married at Ingleshaw Church early
in the new year. I should have preferred Westminster Abbey, and the height of the season; but
George is a person with whom it is quite useless to
argue. He does not intend you to be presented
until after your marriage, which will save trouble,
he says. What an absurd idea! You ought to
have made your hit as one of the beauties of the
season before you were married. It would have
been a *cachet* for you when you began your career as a
wife. But men have no foresight; and my brother
is just forty years behind the day in all his ideas."

"But I would ever so much rather be married
quietly at Ingleshaw than have a grand London
wedding, aunt Ethel," answered Lucille.

"Well, it will save a good deal of money, and
that seems to be all the aristocracy think about
nowadays," said Lady Carlyon contemptuously.

"I am sure *that* is not my father's reason," said
Lucille.

"Perhaps not. Your father was always fond of
hiding his light under a bushel. Give him his worm-
eaten old books and a quiet corner, and he is con-

tent.   And now, Lucille, how about your trousseau?
It is time you began to see about that."

"Dearest aunt, when I don't even know in what
month I am going to be married!   There is plenty
of time."

"There is never plenty of time where dressmakers are concerned," answered Lady Carlyon,
with authority.   "I know what the creatures are,
and how little trust there is to be put in them.   If
you want the best people to work for you, you must
give them good notice."

"Why cannot Miss Sanderson make my gowns,
aunt?   She has done very well for me hitherto."

Miss Sanderson was the chief milliner and man-
tua-maker of Sevenoaks, and was looked up to as a
great authority on Paris fashions.

"My child, you have been in the nursery,"
shrieked Lady Carlyon, "and it did not matter a
straw what you wore.   But do you suppose Miss
Sanderson is the proper person to launch you in
society?   Half a woman's success, nowadays, depends on her dressmaker.   Your gowns fit you well
enough, I allow.   It is really wonderful how these
country dressmakers contrive to fit so well, when a
forty-guinea gown from Regent-street will come home
all wrinkles.   But it is not enough nowadays that a
woman's gowns should fit.   They must be original,

daring. Every new gown should be a new departure. I have been reflecting seriously upon this
matter, and I have come to the conclusion that your
dinner and visiting gowns must be made by Muntzowski."

"What an extraordinary name! Who is Muntzowski?"

"Quite the newest dressmaker in London. She
is a Pole, and a born artist. Forty years ago Balzac
declared that the Slavonic temperament was the
artistic temperament; but this is the first development of the Slavonic mind in dressmaking. Muntzowski's gowns are something *hors ligne*. She has
a feeling for colour, an audacity in her outlines, unknown hitherto. Dressed by Muntzowski you will
be the rage."

"Dear aunt, if you knew how little I care about
my gowns, beyond wearing the colours Bruno likes
best—"

"Don't affect eccentricity, Lucille. It is every
sensible woman's object in life to be dressed better
than her neighbours. In what else can a woman
shine? Can she ever hope to play or sing as well
as the people she can hire? Can she paint as well
as a professional painter? or sit her horse as well
as a country squire's daughter, who only lives to
follow the hounds? A woman of fashion cannot

afford to fritter away her time upon accomplish-
ments. There are two things in which she ought
to be perfect—her gowns and her conversation. I
shall take you up to town next week to see Muntzowski."

Lucille laughed at her aunt's intensity, but promised to do whatever her father desired with regard
to that mountain of new clothes which the feminine
mind considers indispensable to matrimony. It was
natural to her to be gracefully and prettily dressed;
and her own artistic taste had always modified the
fashions which Miss Sanderson recommended to her
notice. To please her father—to please Bruno—
had been her highest ambition; and she could not
imagine a state of being in which the admiration
of the outside world would be of any value to her.

Lady Carlyon heard of her niece's goodness to
Elizabeth May—heard, and disapproved, just as
Miss Marjorum had disapproved. She thought the
scarlet fever was only a just consequence of Lucille's
folly.

"I only hope it will be a lesson which will make
you wiser in the future," she said. "But I am very
sorry to find you have kept the ungrateful minx in
the house."

"It was not her fault I was ill, aunt," remon-

strated Lucille; "and she nursed me devotedly
through my illness."

"Nursed you devotedly, indeed! Artful hussy!
Of course, once having got her nose inside the
Castle, she was eager enough to stay. I saw her in
the corridor the other day, and I didn't at all like
the look of her. Sly, Lucille, sly. The sooner you
get rid of her the better."

"I am sure you misjudge her, aunt," said Lucille, with a troubled look. Her mind had never
been clear about Elizabeth since that night on
board the yacht.

"I never misjudged any one in my life," replied
Lady Carlyon positively. "I always begin by thinking badly of persons of that class; and I have never
been disappointed in the result. What are you going to do with that young woman?"

"I intended her to fill Tompion's place—"

"To take her as your own maid? Absurd!"

"I'm afraid she is too good for that."

"Too good!" shrieked Lady Carlyon. "A creature rescued from the gutter, who has never been
taught hairdressing, and cannot have a notion of
altering a gown—a chit utterly without experience!
What could she do for your figure or your complexion, if either were to give way suddenly?"

Lucille did not enter upon these details. She

hoped that it would be very long before her toilet became a work of art, like her aunt's.

"I have changed my mind about Elizabeth," she said. "She is so intellectual, so quick at learning, so superior in all her ideas, that I think she would do better as a nursery governess. She might begin in that way—teaching young children, and carrying on her own education all the while; and by and by she would be fit for a superior situation."

"O, as a nursery governess—to trudge about country lanes with troublesome children—she might do very well. But that is a way of being buried alive which a young woman with her good looks will not endure long, I'm afraid," added Lady Carlyon.

The return to Ingleshaw had ended the daily, and almost hourly, association between Lady Lucille and her *protégée*. The Earl's presence at the Castle altered the manner of his daughter's life. It was no longer possible for her, had she been so inclined, to have Elizabeth May about her as a companion. Elizabeth fell naturally back into the place which had been at first given to her. She occupied a little room communicating with Tompion's large and airy chamber. She worked industriously at plain sewing, and did any light housework which Tompion could find for her to do. She attended to the flowers in Lady Lucille's rooms, and this, of all tasks, seemed her favourite occupation.

But although she was relegated to the position of a servant, her education still went on. Miss Marjorum had very little to occupy her now that Lady Carlyon was established at the Castle, and was glad to employ her superfluous energies in urging Elizabeth May along the thorny path of culture. She gave three hours a day to the task of tuition, delighted to have so docile a pupil, entranced by the sound of her own voice as she pronounced those Johnsonian sentences which had gone over the heads of so many young scions of patrician trees, but which had never been so meekly and reverently listened to as they were by Elizabeth. The field which had so long been left fallow, this virgin soil of a young untutored mind, now gave the promise of a splendid harvest. Miss Marjorum entered heartily into the notion of Elizabeth's beginning a life of usefulness as a nursery governess.

"It is the most honourable career open to a woman," she said. "It is the one profession which a lady can enter without a blush. The governess can pass through life without overstepping the bounds of maidenly modesty. She need never come in contact with the ruder sex. She is a nun without the restraint of the convent. And under her fostering care are developed the minds of the future. She is the intellectual mother of great men and accomplished women. Many a distinguished *savant* can trace his success in life to the care with which his governess prepared him for Eton. Many a woman of rank owes her social triumphs to the thoroughness with which she was taught her French verbs."

Elizabeth listened with a faint sigh, and a silence which Miss Marjorum took for assent. She was very eager to learn: yet it did not seem to her that an earthly paradise opened before the footsteps of a nursery governess. To walk about the Kentish lanes with little children dragging at her skirts, to sit in a rectory parlour teaching the alphabet or cutting bread-and-butter—well, it would be an honourable drudgery among fair and cleanly surroundings; but it would be no less a drudgery than the old life of the muddy streets and the flower-basket. And in this new life there would be no one to care for her; while in the old life there had been some one who loved her passionately—some one of whom she now thought with a shudder—but whose love had been sweet to her once.

She saw very little of Lady Lucille now, and when they did meet it seemed as if there were a gulf between them. Lucille was kind, but her man-

ner was statelier than it had been. She expressed
an interest in Elizabeth's studies; but the old friendly
warmth, the girlish playfulness which had made
Elizabeth forget that they were not equals, had altogether vanished. One day the girl took courage
to ask if she had offended her patroness.

"No, Elizabeth," Lucille answered gravely; "but
you have disappointed me a little. You remember
what Mr. Challoner said that last night on the
yacht."

"Yes," faltered Elizabeth, with downcast eyes.

"He told me that you were not happy; and then
I saw that my first plan for your life was a mistake.
You could not be as I had fancied, my maid, and
almost my companion. Your jealous temper would
not allow that."

"Only jealous because I love too well," said
Elizabeth, still looking downward, and with a hectic
flush upon her cheeks.

"I do not think that is the best kind of love. I
saw then that I had been mistaken, and that it
would be better that your new life should be inde-
pendent of mine. You take so kindly to education,
and you are so young, that it is only fair your mind
should be allowed to develop itself. As a lady's-
maid you could have very little opportunity for im-

provement; as a governess your education need never stop."

"And when I am old I shall be a kind of learned machine, like Miss Marjorum," said Elizabeth.

"Surely that will be better than selling flowers in the streets," answered Lucille coldly.

"Yes, that was a dreadful life," said the girl, with a faint shudder. "I sometimes look back and wonder how I ever bore it; but when I look forward there seems nothing much worth living forth. Life seems all blank, somehow."

She set down the vase of flowers which she had been arranging, and left the room. Her step was slow and heavy. She had a tired listless air which struck Lucille, whose eyes followed her to the door.

"She is changed in some way," thought Lucille. "I can't understand her."

Now that it was fully understood that Elizabeth May was to be educated, and was to earn her living by and by as a governess, she was no longer obliged to associate with the servants; and this was an infinite relief to her. They were much more respectable, much better mannered, than the riffraff companions of her girlhood; but she had found it harder to get on with them. Their world was not her world. They despised her on account of her antecedents; they disliked her as an interloper, and were utterly unable to recognise that inborn superiority which raised her above them. She had now escaped from all association with the servants, except Tompion, who was more kindly disposed towards her now that she was no longer intended for Lady Lucille's own service. Elizabeth took her meals in the little sitting-room where Tompion worked, in company with a sewing-machine and a bloated spaniel of affectionate temper, which Tompion had reared from puppyhood to asthmatic age. It was a lonely life which she was now leading at Ingleshaw Castle, a life which gave her ample leisure for thought, and for the contemplation of that future which, as she had said, seemed blank and empty.

Sometimes of an afternoon, when she had finished her task of needlework, she would go for a lonely ramble in the park. Lady Lucille had given her leave to go where she liked within the boundary of the fence, which enclosed a space of between six and seven miles in circumference.

It was drawing towards the end of October, and those warm sunshiny days on the blue water seemed to belong to a remote past, when Elizabeth started upon one of these lonely rambles. The sky was a dull gray, and there was a stormy feeling in the air; but Elizabeth was not afraid of bad weather. She had grown very weary of the silence of the corridor outside her lonely room, and even the endearments of the obese spaniel, which insisted upon clambering into her lap, had not been sufficient to beguile her mind of its sadness.

Her steps grew lighter when she was out in the air, under the dull autumn sky. She paused on her way down-stairs to look out of a window from which she could see Lucille, Bruno, and the two girls from the parsonage, playing tennis on the wide level lawn. How bright and gay those figures in pink and blue gowns looked under the gray sky, against the velvety green sward, the warm red wall! What an air of happiness in those quick movements, that light laughter!

"I suppose God meant them to be always happy," she thought; "but I was born different. When I came here I thought I was going to be happy; yes, I was quite happy—as happy as I could be in heaven; and then—"

She ended with a long sigh, and turned impatiently from the window. Her last look at the lawn showed her Bruno talking confidentially to Lucille, as they stood aside in a pause of the game.

The wind was tossing the fir-tree tops when Elizabeth entered the plantation where Lucille found her asleep in the fair May morning. Everything wore a different aspect now. There were hardly any flowers left—a tuft of harebells here and there on a grassy knoll, a belated orchis, a few autumn violets. The firs looked dark and wintry, and every gust swept a shower of yellow leaves from the young oaks. Elizabeth had rambled a long way round the chase before she entered the plantation, and now she sat down to rest almost on the spot where Lucille found her.

"I wonder what would have happened to me if she had not come this way that day? Should I have lain here till I died, or should I have found strength to crawl a little further along the dusty road that leads to the Union? Even then I don't know if they would have taken me in. I should have been only a casual."

She spoke these last words aloud, in a low quiet voice, as she sat listless and meditative, with one ungloved hand straying idly among the bracken on the bank by her side.

"Not much comfort for casuals anywhere, eh, Bess?" said a voice close at hand; and a man, slender, lithe, sinewy, rose with a sudden undulating movement, like a snake, from the deep rank fern.

The girl looked at him with wide bewildered eyes; and, as she looked, every vestige of colour faded out of her face; even the parted lips whitened, as her breath came and went flutteringly.

"Tom, is it you?" she faltered faintly.

"Who should it be? Did you expect Jack—or Joe—or Bill—or Jim?" he asked, with a harsh laugh, gathering himself into a sitting position upon the bank, and stretching out a sinuous arm with the evident intention of encircling the girl's waist; but she drew herself suddenly away, with an angry look in her dark eyes.

"What's the matter, my lass? Sure to goodness, you're not going to turn your back upon me because you're up in the world, and I'm down!"

"You left me to starve," answered Bess, with lowered eyelids, sitting as far from him as the bank allowed, her attitude and countenance distinctly expressive of abhorrence; "I don't quarrel with you for that. Perhaps you couldn't help it; perhaps you didn't care. But when you left me once, you left me for ever. You and I had done with each other."

"No, we hadn't, lady fair," said the man, looking up at her from his lower place, with a cunning grin. "It might have been so if I'd had my way. But you and your pal, the city missionary, worked it out different. You wanted all things correct and reg'lar—church and parson; love, honour, and obey, and all the usual patter; and, by the living Jingo, you shall obey!"

"I should have died in this wood, if it hadn't been for the young lady who found me, and took me to her beautiful home, and brought me back to life by her kindness," said Elizabeth, still looking downward, staring sullenly at the grass, with its infinite variety of hue, from green to russet.

"Yes, and pampered you, and made a fool of you, and had you taught to play the lady," sneered the man. "I know all about it."

"How do you know?"

"Because I'm not a fool, and am used to keep my eyes and my ears open. I've been on the tramp for the last three weeks, and it was only yesterday as I dropped into this blooming bit of country, and stopped for a meal of victuals at the Cat and Fiddle —a neat little old-fashioned sort of a pub at the end of the village. The rum cull of the casa happens to be a friendly sort of a chap—very free with the patter; so I let him jaw. I asked him a few leading questions about that blooming Castle over there, which I could see the tops of the towers over the trees, like a scene at the poor old Vic.; and he jawed no end about the Hurl, and the young lady, and how she was the most charitable young lady as never was, and how she'd picked up a beautiful young creetur in the wood, at death's door, and had took her home, and kind of 'dopted her like—a pore young thing as was on the tramp to jine her sweetheart at Dover. Now I can't say if it was the mention of Dover, or whether it was the old Cat and Fiddle's patter about your good looks, and your black eyes, and your name o' Bess, which he dropped promiscuous, that put me up to trap; but it comed into my blessed noddle that this young 'ooman was my gal, and none other."

The landlord of the Cat and Fiddle was Tompion's maternal uncle, and Tompion's evenings out were sometimes spent in the private parlour of that rustic inn; so Bess was not surprised at the publican's readiness to talk about Ingleshaw Castle and its inhabitants.

"So I makes up my mind to hang out at the Cat and Fiddle for a night," pursued Tom, sprawling at ease upon the bank, "and I loafs about to-day till I falls in with you. I've been up at the Castle and had a look about me, and I heerd there as you was fond of walking alone in the woods; so I prowled about here till I seed you; and an uncommon chilly welcome I've got for my pains."

"What do you want with me?" asked the girl sullenly, flashing one angry glance at him and letting her eyelids fall again, as if she had looked at something hateful. "You beat me."

"Only when I was mad with the drink, my lass."

"Mad with drink? yes. You spent the money upon which we might have lived a decent life—like Christians, or at any rate like human beings—on drink that changed you into a savage. You made me work for you as well as for myself. You let me starve, and you left me."

"Only when I'd got into trouble, and London was too hot to hold me."

"You told me you'd enlisted, and that your regiment was going to India."

"There was a touch of romance in that, Bess. I thought you was hard on me, and I wanted to melt your stubborn heart. . I had some thoughts of taking the Queen's shilling when I left London, but I thought better of it on reflection. Liberty's worth more than a bob, and I had no fancy for the guard-room or the cat."

"You told me nothing but lies, then? You never went to Dover?"

"Not any nearer than Rochester. I've been working in a circle within thirty or forty mile of London."

"What kind of work have you been doing?"

The man looked meditative, felt in his pockets

for a short pipe, found it, filled it, lighted it, and then replied carelessly,

"Odd jobs—anythink.   You know I'm pretty handy."

"Stable-work?" interrogated Elizabeth.

"Partly stables.   A fellow that's down on his luck can't afford to be particklar.   And now tell me what kind of a berth you've got up yonder.   It was like your luck to drop into such quarters.   And, O scissors, ain't we smart!   A brand-new black gound as fits us like our skin, and sech ladylike boots! Blest if ever I knowed you'd such a pretty foot, Bess!" he added, looking admiringly at the slender foot with its well-developed instep, which Bess tucked under her gown with an angry movement as he spoke.

"Well, I'm blowed!   That's the first time I knowed it was high treason for a husband to admire his wife's foot," exclaimed Tom Brook, with an injured air.   "All I can say is, as I said afore, it was like your luck to get free quarters at Ingle-shaw Castle."

"It was the first good luck that ever came my way: and now I suppose you've come to spoil it all."

"No, I ain't.   I'm not such a selfish beggar as that.   I'm not agoing to say, 'Bess, you're my wife, and if I must tramp the country, you must pad the hoof alongside o' me.' No, you've got a good home, and you'd better stick to it as long as ever you can. But I want you to bear in mind all the same as I'm your husband, and to be civil and pleasant spoken when you and me meet promiscuous, as we have this afternoon."

"You mean that you are to hang about this place, and that I am to meet you—secretly?" she asked.

"I don't know what you mean by hanging about. If I find I can get a job of work in the village, I shall stay; if I can't—"

A knowledge of certain dark antecedents in Mr. Brook's early life—escapades which in his class of life had counted only as the wild oats of youthful indiscretion, and of which Bess herself had thought lightly enough when she married him—now inclined her to suspect his motives.

"What work can there be for you in such a place as Ingleshaw village?" she asked.

"There's always work for me where there's horses," answered Tom Brook. "I'll get somethin' to do, don't you be afeard; and I won't spile your little game. You shall play the lady up at the Castle for the next six months, if yer like, till I've made a potful of money, and can come and claim yer, with a good coat on my back and a top 'at on my 'ed, like a born gentleman. But you'll have to bear in mind you're my wife, and be civil and obedient in the mean time, my lady. I'm not going to stand any gammon."

His wife looked at him with eyes in which dark fires of scorn and hate were strangely blended. She hardly knew herself, in that moment, whether she most despised or most hated him. Yet she had loved him once, or believed she loved him, when, of all the brutes among whom she herded, this brute alone had shown a touch of kindness and pity for her, and had cherished her, after his rough fashion, with a feeling which was not altogether brutal.

But now—now that her ears had grown used to another language, that her eyes had looked upon another race—the face and the voice, the tones, the movements of this man, who was by law her master, inspired such aversion, such an infinite, unspeakable loathing as she had never felt in her life before— no, not for the vilest of that vile herd in which she had been born and reared. She was a creature of strong feelings; one of those fierce tropical natures which crop up now and then among the sober northern races. Her love and her hatred had ever been more intense than other people's; and now she shrank shuddering and abhorrent from the man whose caress had once seemed a friendly shelter.

"You left me of your own accord," she said, in low resolute tones. He could hear the change in her accentuation, just as he could see the refinement of her appearance—every line softened, every hue more delicate than in the old days. "You lied to me of your own accord. I followed you—as far as I could go—on the road to Dover, dying of hunger all the while; followed you till I fell down in this wood, and never thought to get up again. You left me in the workhouse infirmary, dying, as you were told. You sent me a scrap of a letter to say you had enlisted, and were going to Dover with a regiment that was under orders for India in two month's time. When I got round again, you told me I must get on as best I might till better times—when you should have served your time, and could come back to London and make a home for me. That was all falsehood from beginning to end. You only wanted to get rid of me—civilly. And now I want to get rid of you—civilly. I will live the rest of my life alone, remembering that I am a married woman, for the sake of my promise in the church; but I will never acknowledge you as my husband, or live with you as your wife."

She confronted him steadily as she spoke, looked

him through and through, and defied him, every
feature in her grand and beautiful face rigid with
the intensity of her feeling. No man, looking at
her, could doubt that she meant what she said, and
would carry out her resolve to the bitter end.

"Won't you, my lady!" exclaimed Mr. Brook,
scowling at her savagely, but with a half-timorous
irresolution in his looks, as of one not quite prepared to cope with this fiery spirit. "We'll see if
we can't compel yer. The law's uncommon hard
upon husbands and wives when they go for to shirk
their 'sponsabilities. You'll find the law come down
upon you heavy, if I once say the word."

"But you won't say the word. You daren't go
to Lord Ingleshaw, and say, 'I'm an honest man,
and that woman is my wife.' You daren't face him.
He's a county magistrate, and the kind of man to
read you like an open book."

"Who said I was going to Lord Ingleshaw?" exclaimed the man, with a sudden change of tone;
"not that I'm afeared o' yer Lord Ingleshaws, or
any other blessed old blokes of the same stamp.
I've held their 'osses afore now, when I've been
down on my luck, outside o' the Hadmirality or the
'Orse Guards, and I know what shaky old coves
they is—gone at the knees and weak in the pastern-
jints. Didn't I say as I wasn't goin' to spile yer

game? I only wants a bit o' civility and friendly
feelin', for the sake o' old long Sims, as we say in
the classics. Come, old gal, be civil to a feller, and
tell us what you've been a-doin' of all this time."

So addressed, Bess relented a little. The hard
lines about her mouth relaxed, the darkly brooding
eyes shed a gentler light. She told her husband
briefly how she had been saved from death by Lady
Lucille's Christian charity, and made a new creature
by her generous affection.

"Well, she must be uncommon green," remarked
Mr. Brook at the close of this narration, "to pick up
a young woman as might have been a regular old
hand—an out-and-out gaol-bird—and to take her
into sech a house as Ingleshaw Castle, and give her
the run of the place! And I suppose there's as
much silver there—in the way of forks and spoons,
and tea-urns and dish-covers, and sechlike—as would
stock a silversmith's shop."

"There is everything beautiful in the house; but
Lady Lucille cares more for flowers and china, and
books and music, than for all the silver in the world;
and so do I."

"Ah, that's the way with young women. They're
jest like children, caught by pretty colours what
strikes the eye. But if I was a nobleman, I'd have
my dinin'-table a mask of solid silver jugs and

tankards, and dish-covers and butter-boats, and sech-like. I'd never eat off anything but silver; and I make no doubt Lord Ingleshaw eats his victuals off solid silver every day of his blessed old life."

"I don't know," answered Bess indifferently; "but I shouldn't think it likely. He's a very simple-minded gentleman, plain in all his ways; but he is a gentleman. I never knew what the word meant till I saw him—and one other."

"Ah, I knows the kind o' bloke," said Mr. Brook, with an astute air—"fine spread o' shirt-front and shepherd's-plaid kickseys, a gold-'eaded cane and a double-barrelled heyeglass. And now tell us all about the 'ouse; a reg'lar harmy o' servants, I'll be bound; all eatin' their 'eads off, like pampered 'osses."

Bess did not tell him the number of the servants; nor did she gratify him with any details as to the interior arrangements of the Castle. Her suspicions had been aroused by his eagerness upon the subject of the Ingleshaw plate. She had never known him concerned in actual crime; but she knew that his interpretation of the law of property was easy, not to say loose; and she was determined to give him as little information as possible—only so much, in fact, as he could wring from her by persistent questioning. Nor, when he persisted in a course of in-

quiry which seemed suspicious, did she hesitate to
give him misleading answers.

He was too acute, too thoroughly steeped in
cunning, not to see that she was deceiving him; but
he did not broadly accuse her of falsehood. He
heard her with a mocking twinkle in his rat-like
eyes, whistled a snatch of the last popular melody
which had thrilled the music-halls of Bermondsey,
cocked his hat over his brow, and pocketed his
empty pipe, as he rose from the bank where he had
been reposing.

"That'll do," he said. "Ta-ta, my lass. When
I want to look you up, I shall know where to find
you."

He walked slowly away without another word,
vanishing among the dark straight fir-trunks into dim
leafy distance, leaving Elizabeth May still seated,
drawn close up against the tree, as she had drawn
herself when first he approached, instinctively shrink-
ing from him.

She sat pale, motionless, with fixed eyes, while
the light faded, and umber and purple shadows
thickened in the dimness under the trees. She sat
there till she looked only a dark blotch upon the
dusk of the woodland. Yet, thus seated, thus faintly
distinguishable, she was seen by a man who came
sauntering along the narrow woodland path smoking

a cigarette. He came close to her, bent over her, looked her full in the face; she looking up at him with agonised eyes, but never stirring.

"Elizabeth, what is the matter? why are you sitting here alone in the dark?"

He had questioned her once before about herself and her own feelings—that night on board the yacht—and had got nothing for his pains but tears and a passionate protest against Fate—broken burning words, which had stirred some strange half-dormant passion within him, which thrilled responsive to that subtle unexpressed passion in her. On that fatal night he had known that she loved him: and he had known as certainly that he loved her. From that hour to this they had never spoken to each other, had avoided each other's path as much as possible, or had met and passed with averted looks, or that blank icy stare which sees nothing.

"Elizabeth, what has happened?" he asked; and the unconscious tenderness of his tone moved her like sweetest music.

"Not very much. I have been brought face to face with my old life, that is all."

The tears welled into her eyes and poured down her ashen cheeks; her breast heaved with passionate sobs. That sympathetic voice of Bruno's had loosened the fountain. Till now she had hardened her heart to bear her burden; but his sympathy was more than she could bear.

"You have heard something, or seen some one," he speculated. "How white you are, and your hands are icy cold!" touching them as they lay loosely clasped in her lap. "Elizabeth, you are crying!"

The sight of her tears made him forget everything. Another moment—a moment in which his heart beat like a sledge-hammer—he was sitting by her side upon the bank, his arm round her waist, her head resting on his shoulder.

"My dear one, I would give my life to comfort you!" he cried passionately.

Only for a moment did she rest in that embrace, and yet it seemed to her as if she had been lifted into the empyrean, as if she were in a diviner, purer world, where nothing less than perfect joy could live; felt as Helen may feel, resting in the arms of Achilles, in that sacred isle where death dwells not—perfect beauty, perfect manhood, courage, honour inviolate, linked for ever in immortal union. Only for a moment did Bess abandon herself to that entrancing dream of loving and being beloved by him who was to her as godlike as Achilles; and then she remembered who he was, and who she was, and that this earth around and about them was no fair shadowland, in which the miracles of love may triumph over the hard facts of destiny.

"You forget yourself, Mr. Challoner," she said quietly, slipping from his encircling arm, which loosened and released her readily enough.

Yes, for an instant he had forgotten himself, and Fate, and that dear girl who three months ago had filled his life with gladness by the frank avowal of her love. And now, sitting here in the gloaming, looking into those dark eyes, hearing that low thrilling voice, the love of his boyhood and his youth seemed to him as a bondage and a slavery, from which death would be a cheap deliverance.

"Yes, I have been brought back to the thought of my old life," pursued Elizabeth, with quiet gravity, "and of what I was before Lady Lucille saved me —of how I spoke, and looked, and thought even; for I don't suppose I was any better than other people among whom I lived."

"You were better: you could never have been like them. You were among them, but not of them," protested Bruno.

"Well, perhaps I may have been a little less vulgar than the man I saw to-day."

"What man?"

"My husband."

"Your husband!"

"Yes; I am a double-dyed impostor, am I not?" said the girl, with a bitter laugh. "When Lord Ingleshaw questioned me about my past life, I was afraid to tell him I was a married woman, for fear he should refuse to let me stay at the Castle, and should want to send me on my way, with a few pounds in my pocket perhaps, to look for my husband; so I told him Tom Brook was my sweetheart."

"And Tom Brook is your husband?" asked Bruno slowly, as if every word cost him an effort.

"Yes."

"Would it be too much to ask who he is—what manner of man?"

"A scamp—a vagabond—a man who works in stables and cab-yards, but who lives by his wits mostly. He was kind to me once, when everybody else in the world was rough and cruel. When I was lying ill in a garret, alone all day long—for the girls who shared my room were out at the factories where they worked—Tom Brook came to look after me; brought me a couple of oranges, or a bunch of cheap grapes, when my lips were parched with fever; sat beside me and talked to me; and I was grateful to him. He was the first man who ever treated me kindly. Even such rough kindness as his was sweet—it was so new. When I got better he followed me about, and wanted to be my sweetheart. Once, when a man was rude to me in the street—one Saturday night—the kind of man we used to call a swell, Tom Brook knocked him down. On Sundays he used to come to tea with the other girls and me, and used to take us for walks, and give us coffee or ices at the little Italian shops round about. Sometimes he took me to the play; and then one morning he told me that he'd got the City missionary to speak to the parson, and that the banns had been given out for the last three Sundays, and he and I were to be married. We went straight to the church with the missionary, who gave me away, and signed the book in the vestry. He was a good old man, and I should have been a better woman if I had listened better to his teaching, and tried to read my Bible; but perhaps, if you knew what life is like in the alley where I lived, you wouldn't wonder that I didn't do it."

"And so you became Mrs. Thomas Brook," said Bruno, in biting tones. His whole nature seemed hardened by the idea of this marriage. "I hope you were happy in your domestic relations."

"Happy! Well, I had some one who belonged to me—a strong arm to knock down anybody who tried to insult me. I wasn't quite such a forlorn creature as I had been; but I was a slave, and I

Flower and Weed.   11

had a hard master. When he was sober he made
me wait upon him hand and foot; when he was
drunk he beat me. When he got tired of his work,
and the kind of life he was leading, he left me—
left me when I had most need of his kindness, for
I was lying at death's door in the infirmary at the
Union. You know what happened to me when I
came out of the Union."

"How did he come here to-day?"

"He heard of me at the village inn, and waited
about here to see me."

"Did he want to take you away with him?"

"No; but he says he shall claim me by and by,
when he is better off. O Mr. Challoner, can he
claim me—has he the power to take me away with
him?"

"He is your husband. That is a position of
some strength; and no doubt you are fond of him.
You would not refuse to share his home and his
fortunes."

"I would kill myself sooner than acknowledge
any right of his over me."

The pale steadfast face, the light in the fixed
eyes, told that this was no empty threat.

Bruno sighed heavily, and sat staring at the
ground.

"Yet you liked him once," he said meditatively —"liked him well enough to marry him."

"That was when I was in utter darkness, God help me!—when I thought he was better than other men—just as a man set upon by wolves would hail a dog as his friend. Those other men I knew were like wolves."

"Poor soul, poor soul!" sighed Bruno. "Well, I'll tell Lord Ingleshaw your pitiful story, and he will help you to keep this husband of yours at a distance. You should have told his lordship the truth in the first instance. It would have been better."

"Yes, I know that now. I was too cowardly then to tell the truth; but now I would sooner cut my tongue out than tell Lord Ingleshaw a lie."

"That's well, Elizabeth. God meant you to be noble and stanch and loyal—God made you brave as well as beautiful. And now you had best hurry home before it grows dark. Shake hands. Don't be afraid. I was a madman just now; but all that is past and gone. We both mean to be true."

He held out his hand—they two standing face to face in the autumn twilight—and she put her own hand into his. Both hands were deadly cold, but they clasped each other with a clasp that meant self-respect, loyalty to Lucille, and that highest of all human virtues—a stern adherence to difficult duty. And thus they parted: Elizabeth walking quickly back to the Castle; Bruno lighting another cigar, and sauntering further into the darkness of the wood.

———

CHAPTER VI.

A LONELY LIFE.

"Kisse me, quod she, we be no longer wrothe."

It was quite dark before Elizabeth arrived at the Castle, and the long range of windows on the first floor shone with the soft light of lamps and wax-candles, and here and there the ruddier glow of a fire. It looked like that fairy castle which Elizabeth had read of in those familiar tales of witch and goblin which had been her easy introduction to the realm of poetic literature. A pleasant place to live in—a happy and wonderful house, as compared with that dim dwelling in the gloom of a fetid alley to which Elizabeth had been wont to return at this season last year. Yet, such a strange intangible thing is happiness that she went back to that old historic mansion with a heart as heavy as that she had carried to her lodging in the London slum. She had learnt the mystery of new pains and sorrows, new needs and longings, which reached beyond the region of every-day wants. She had known the pangs of Lazarus, and in the

days of her poverty had envied the rich, thinking
it impossible for them to suffer; and now she knew
that Dives has his gnawing canker, his troubled
slumbers, his sorrowful dreams, as well as Lazarus.

Elizabeth went round by the stable-yard on her
way to the Castle, not caring to enter by that imposing doorway which would bring her face to face
with the porter and the groom of the chambers.
She wanted to go in without being seen by any
one, if it were possible. There was a small door
in a turret, which opened on a winding stair that
led up to the corridor close to Tompion's rooms,
and towards this door Elizabeth directed her steps.
She passed two men standing near the yard-gates,
in confidential conversation; and she hurried on
with fluttering heart and quickened steps, for one
of those men was Tom Brook. She scarcely drew
breath till she was in her own little room, inside
Tompion's; and then she sat down with a beating
heart, and began to wonder what Brook and the
groom could have found to talk about, and whether
she was the subject of their conversation. She felt
that Brook's presence in the stable-yard meant evil
to her—that he was dogging her footsteps with
some malicious intent, in spite of his promise not
to interfere with her good fortune. She had defied
him, when it would perhaps have been wiser to

conciliate him; but for her very life she could not have cringed to him, or affected any regard for him. If he was to be her foe, she must bear his enmity. Better that than his friendship.

She received a summons to the library soon after breakfast next morning; and, for the second time in her life, she found herself alone with Lord Ingleshaw. He had heard her story from Bruno. He reproved her gently for her want of candour about Tom Brook.

"You told me a falsehood," he said, "when truth would have served your purpose much better; and I hardly know whether I ought to believe you now."

"You may believe me, my lord," she answered, looking at him with such pathetic earnestness that he could not find it in his heart to doubt her. "Think what a lost ignorant creature I was whe In first stood in this room, face to face with you, as I stand to-day. I scarcely knew right from wrong. But since that day your daughter has taught me a great deal. She has taught me to read the Gospel, and to believe in it and love it. She has taught me my duty to God and man."

"If you have learned as much as that in less than six months, you have learned more than many of our greatest philosophers have compassed in a

lifetime," said Lord Ingleshaw, smiling at her
earnestness. "Well, Elizabeth, if this husband of
yours is a brute, you shall not be forced to live
with him; I'll answer for that. So go about your
daily work with a contented spirit, and fear nothing."

"Thank you, my lord. I will try to be worthy
of your kindness," the girl answered meekly. "But
there is one thing I ought to tell you. Tom Brook
was in the stable-yard last night, talking to one of
the grooms. I saw him as I came in. I don't
know that he had any evil intention; but I thought
I ought to tell you."

"Quite right. To which of the men was he
talking?"

"I believe it was Compton, my lord."

"Very good; I'll speak to Compton. When you
told me this Tom Brook was your sweetheart, you
said he was an honest lad, and had never been in
prison. Was that true?"

"Quite true that he was never in prison, my
lord, to my knowledge. But he had companions
and friends that I didn't like. Some of them had
been in prison. The men who hang about a horse-
dealer's yard—"

"Are not the noblest members of our race,"
interrupted his lordship; "I am quite sure of that.

But you have no reason to suppose that your husband belonged to the criminal classes—that he had
ever been concerned in a burglary?"

"No, my lord."

"That will do."

Elizabeth curtsied and withdrew, and Lord
Ingleshaw went out to the stables, inspected his
stud, and took occasion, *en passant*, to interrogate
Compton, who was either very stupid or very artful,
and could give no further account of his interview
with Tom Brook than that he had been standing
at the yard-gate, and the man had asked him to
direct him back to the village. He had lost his
way in the park, and did not know how to regain
the high-road; which, from the geography of the
place, showed a curious lack of intelligence on the
part of the inquirer.

Time passed, and nothing more was seen or
heard of Tom Brook. Elizabeth pursued her studies
—improved herself in a plain English education,
and in the use of the needle and sewing-machine
—in the peaceful solitude of Tompion's sitting-
room. It ought to have been a life of placid and
perfect contentment for one whose earlier years had
been full of toil and trouble; but, if Elizabeth May
was happy, her physical nature did not thrive upon
happiness. Her cheeks grew hollow, and the only

colour that ever came into them now was a hectic scarlet, which glowed and faded with every sudden emotion. Her eyes had a feverish light, and the tall graceful figure, which had rounded to womanly perfection in the summer, had now fallen away to palpable attenuation.

Tompion complained of Elizabeth's daintiness, and made it an offence in this young person that she had not a better appetite for the liberal fare of Ingleshaw Castle.

"It's always the way," said Tompion, waxing confidential over the tea-tray in the housekeeper's room. "Set a beggar on horseback, and we all know where he'll ride. It makes me quite ill to see her dinner sent away, just mucked about a bit, but none of it eaten."

"Perhaps she is ill," suggested Mrs. Prince, the housekeeper, who was a fat kindly creature, and meant well to everybody, so long as no one wanted to dig her out of her armchair.

"Lor', no; she's well enough. It's nothing but airs and graces," retorted Tompion. "She's in the sulks because Lady Lucille don't take so much notice of her now that she's got her aunt and Mr. Challoner to occupy her time."

"And the poor thing feels being taken up for pastime, and then let drop again," said the housekeeper. "Well, I don't much wonder at that; I shouldn't like it myself."

"*You* wouldn't, of course, Mrs. Prince; no more should I," replied Tompion, with a dignified air; "but such dirt as that oughtn't to be particular. She ought never to have been brought into such a house as this; but, being brought in through my young lady's mistaken kindness, she ought to be too thankful for all that's done for her. Nursery governess, indeed! a pretty kind of person to teach gentlefolks' children! You should have seen the rags I took off her back the day Lady Lucille found her."

"They were clean," said the housekeeper; "that's something to her credit. And I must say she has a natural gentility about her that has often made me wonder—and that quick at learning! Miss Marjorum says she never met her equal."

"Miss Marjorum is an old fool," protested Tompion, purple with jealousy, "and so fond of teaching that she would teach a cow, if there was nothing else in the way to be taught."

"She never taught you, Tompion," said the butler, grinning.

"I should think not, indeed!" ejaculated the damsel, with a contemptuous toss of her head; "I

should like to see her take such a liberty! Old
Marjorum knows her place better than that."

Elizabeth, disliked by the servants, and left to
her own resources by Lady Lucille, led a life that
was passing lonely; and it is not in solitude that
weak humanity can best cure those inward fevers
which consume the soul and fret the nerves. In
Byron's familiar phrase, Elizabeth was eating her
own heart in that dull and placid life at Ingleshaw.
On many an October afternoon, as she wandered
far afield in her solitary walk, she had thought it
would have been better for her to be toiling with
yonder rough and noisy hop-pickers, resting after
the long day's labour amongst that rough herd
under the stars, with a stone for her pillow, like
Jacob, than to live in the lap of luxury at Ingleshaw
Castle.

Yet there were moments when she felt a thrill
of pride and delight at realising the change in
herself, physical, mental, moral, remembering what
she had been, and seeing what she was. Once,
when she had dusted the china and arranged the
flowers in Lady Lucille's dressing-room, she paused
for a minute, startled by her own reflection in the
cheval-glass—the tall slim figure, the neatly-fitting
gown, the refined look, the graceful carriage.

"I don't think any one would know I had been picked up out of the dirt," she said to herself, proud of her own beauty, which had acquired the crowning charm of refinement. And yet the glory of freshness and colour was gone, and it looked a fragile fading beauty, as of one doomed to an early grave.

One day Lucille was struck by the change in her *protégée*, and questioned her closely about her health. Elizabeth would not admit that she was ill. She owned to feeling tired sometimes, and to sleeping badly; and that was all. Lucille was kinder to her, more friendly and familiar, that day than she had been for a long time.

"Mrs. Raymond is going to Brighton with her children soon after Christmas," said Lucille. "It would be nice for you to go with her, and get accustomed to the family and to your new duties. The change of air would do you good. I believe it is change you want."

Mrs. Raymond was the wife of Lord Ingleshaw's land-steward—a bright pleasant little woman, who had shown some interest in Elizabeth's history, and had volunteered, knowing that history, to take her as nursery governess for her young brood, so soon as Elizabeth should be competent for the post.

"I am not a bit afraid of her antecedents," said

Mrs. Raymond, "for, as my children and their governess are hardly ever out of my sight, I cannot very well be taken in. I shall be able to read Elizabeth like an open book before she has been with me a fortnight."

Elizabeth accepted this future engagement with Mrs. Raymond as her fate, allotted to her by the benefactress to whom she owed everything. She had been introduced to Mrs. Raymond's three chubby daughters and one chubby son, the youngest of the brood, and talked of everywhere emphatically as "the baby," a proud distinction which he merited in somewise by being the fattest and healthiest two-year-old infant in the parish of Ingleshaw. Elizabeth was not fond of children; but she was constrained to admit that, as children go, Mrs. Raymond's off-spring were favourable specimens. They were pictures of health and cleanliness, always prettily and sensibly clad, amiable and sociable in their manners, and with more than the average amount of intelligence. Elizabeth felt that if her life was to be spent with children, it could hardly be better spent than in the Raymond nursery. Mrs. Raymond had always treated her with particular friend-liness; while Mr. Raymond was one of those delight-ful and easy-going husbands who are only at home at meal-times. He passed his days in a light dogcart, driving about the Ingleshaw estate, or going journeys in quest of prize cattle.

Elizabeth was touched by Lady Lucille's interest in her health; but the idea of a change to Brighton had no exhilarating effect upon her.

"You'd like to go, wouldn't you?" asked Lucille, vexed at her indifference. "Brighton is a charming winter place—so gay and smart, and with such lovely shops. You have never seen anything like it. Wouldn't you be pleased if Mrs. Raymond could manage to take you?"

"I don't care about it—much," faltered Elizabeth. "But of course I would go if you wished it, Lady Lucille."

"What wish can I have about it, except for your sake?" exclaimed Lucille, provoked at a coldness which seemed inexplicable: "you seem to care for nothing, to be interested in nothing."

"Yes, yes, I do care for something, with all my heart," cried Elizabeth eagerly, falling on her knees and clasping Lucille's hands and kissing them passionately. "I care for you. I want you to love me and trust me as you did once—before—"

"Before what?" asked Lucille, looking down at her with intent questioning eyes. The two women looked into each other's faces, as if their two souls were giving up their secrets, each to each.

"Before that night on the yacht, when I was weak and wicked, and complained to Mr. Challoner of my fate—I who had so much reason to be grateful to Providence and to you. I have grown wiser since then, Lady Lucille. I have learned to govern my jealous temper, to be thankful for the blessings of my life; and when I am with Mrs. Raymond I mean to work very hard, and to be the best governess her children ever had."

"I believe it is in your power to be anything you like," said Lucille, touched by her earnestness, and ready to repent that half-defined suspicion which had turned her heart from Elizabeth.

She raised the girl from her knees and kissed her, for the first time in her life.

"If ever I forget that kiss or am unworthy of it, let me be remembered as Judas was remembered," said Elizabeth; and from this time her intercourse with Lady Lucille resumed much of its original friendliness, to Tompion's inexpressible disgust.

This was in December, when the park and chase were white with snow, and the drifts were lying deep in all the hollows. Inside the Castle all was warmth and brightness, wood-fires glowing on the wide old hearthstones, and the brazen dogs glittering and flashing in the firelight, while the odours of hot-house flowers, roses, mignonette, hyacinths, lilies of the valley, were intensified by the warmth of the rooms.

"The last snow I remember changed to mud and slush half an hour after it fell," said Elizabeth, "and the last cold winds I remember seemed to blow straight at my bones. Winter means quite a different thing for the rich from what it means for the poor."

The poor were not forgotten by Lucille in that hard weather. She was full of thought for them, full of anxiety to help them. She made Elizabeth her assistant in all her charities, and the girl's knowledge of the needs of the poor, their ways, their prejudices even, was of much use to her. Elizabeth was indefatigable in trudging from cottage to cottage, in visiting the sick. She sat up for several nights with a girl who was dying of consumption, and nursed her as if she had been a sister. Her conduct was so excellent at this period that Lucille put aside that old painful suspicion as an unworthy doubt, and gave Elizabeth her complete confidence. Bruno was absent at this time on an electioneering expedition to a borough in the North of England, with Lord Ingleshaw, and Lucille had leisure to devote herself to the care of her poor. She had cared for them and ministered to them from her childhood upwards; but just now, at the approach of Christmas, she had special duties to perform. And she wished this particular Christmastide to be a golden memory for all the poor in Ingleshaw parish, inasmuch as her own cup of joy was full to overflowing.

Nothing had been heard of Tom Brook since that October twilight, and Elizabeth began to think of her interview with him almost as if it had been a bad dream. It belonged to the past, and had brought no evil consequences.

She seemed happier—nay, she was happier—now than she had been for a long time. Restored to her benefactress's favour, and able to make herself useful as Lucille's almoner, winning many a blessing from the sick and the aged whom her daily visits cheered and comforted, she no longer felt that life was blank and empty. Bruno's absence was a relief to her. She was no longer troubled by the dread of meeting him suddenly in the corridor or in the garden; no longer startled by the sound of his voice in the distance. Her life was more peaceful without that disturbing element. But he was to return for Christmas, and Christmas was drawing near.

Lady Carlyon had departed to another of her

happy hunting-grounds—a fine old abbey in the Midlands, at which Christmas was kept in a much more fashionable and festive manner than at Ingleshaw; where the greatest excitement provided for that season was the tea for the mothers, aunts, and school-children, and the supper for the men and youths in the great mediæval hall. At the Abbey there were to be amateur theatricals and a fancy ball. Lady Carlyon was full of plans for her costume for the ball—which was to be wonderfully effective, and to cost a mere nothing—and she had an idea of performing in one of the plays, if people were very pressing. She went away in the highest spirits, pledging herself to return at least a week before the wedding.

"Every detail of your trousseau is arranged," she said. "I can leave with an easy conscience."

When she was gone Lucille resumed all her old girlish habits, read Italian with Miss Marjorum, practised a great deal, rambled in the park, visited in the village, and made a companion of Elizabeth. Mrs. Raymond and her babies came to afternoon tea in the old schoolroom, in order that Elizabeth —Miss May, as the steward's wife called her— might get used to her future charges. Altogether, it was a social and happy time; and when Elizabeth thought of her position and her surroundings a year ago, and of the drunken brawling which was the only distinguishing mark of the Christmas season in Ramshackle-court, she lifted up her heart in thankfulness for the blessed change.

"There is something very sweet about that girl," said Mrs. Raymond to Lucille, after tea, when Elizabeth had retired to the corridor to play hide-and-seek with Dotty, Totty, Lotty, and the fat baby. "I really think you found a pearl that day in the wood, Lady Lucille."

"Yes," answered Lucille, with a faint sigh; "I know that she has a noble nature. She is so self-sacrificing, so good to the poor. And yet there is a mystery about her which sometimes worries me. I can't quite understand her."

"Dear Lady Lucille, the noblest natures are apt to have hidden depths," answered Mrs. Raymond; "and one must consider this girl's bringing up. I daresay there are times when the memory of old miseries weighs her down—makes her irritable, perhaps. And then she has not a relative in the world. She may feel her loneliness more than we suppose, seeing other people with so many ties. I shall do my best to make her happy when she comes to me; but it will be a great change from the Castle to the Dower House."

Mr. and Mrs. Raymond occupied a charming

old house near the park-gates, which in former days
had been the portion of the dowagers of Ingleshaw;
but which the more frisky dowagers of the present
era would have voted the abomination of desolation.
It was a roomy, rambling, half-timbered edifice,
smothered with roses planted by an old-world
dowager, and with an idyllic garden and orchard.

"I think Elizabeth will be ever so much happier
at the Dower House than she is here," said Lucille.
"She will have more to do, and a more settled
position."

"Well, here I grant she is a little like Mahomet's
coffin, suspended between heaven and earth," as-
sented Mrs. Raymond laughingly. "She will have
a livelier life with us; for Totty, Dotty, and Lotty
are most amusing children. They really do say
such extraordinary things that one can never feel
dull in their company," pursued the fond parent.
"They are so witty that I sometimes catch myself
wondering that I can be their mother. And I'm
sure they don't inherit their comic ideas from
George, for one has to go over a joke three times
to make him understand it."

Being so well disposed towards Elizabeth, Mrs.
Raymond readily consented to take her to Brighton
with the children, when they went there for their
winter holiday; so it was settled that Miss May's

duties were to begin at that time, and her association with Ingleshaw Castle, save as an occasional
visitor to her benefactress, would then come to an
end.

Bruno and Lucille were to be married on the
20th of January, at which time Mrs. Raymond and
her family would be still at Brighton. The Raymonds had not been invited to the wedding, which
was to be attended by none but relations, with the
single exception of Miss Marjorum, who almost
ranked as a relation.

CHAPTER VII.

NOT DISLOYAL.

"Irene, I have loved you, as men love
  Light, music, odour, beauty, love itself;
  Whatever is apart from, and above,
  Those daily needs which deal with dust and pelf."

"Christmas is coming, and Bruno," exclaimed Lucille, on the morning of Christmas-eve, as she worked with Miss Marjorum, Tompion, and Elizabeth May at the decoration of hall, staircase, and corridor. Lord Ingleshaw objected to holly and ivy in the rooms in which he lived—clocks and lamps and picture-frames embowered in greenery gave him an uncomfortable feeling.

"Make the hall and corridor as festive as you please, my dear," he said, "but don't let me see a Madonna by Guido staring at me like an owl out of an ivy-bush, or my Sèvres china made a mere vehicle for the exhibition of holly-berries."

"It may be vulgar, old-fashioned, Philistine," said Lucille, as she twisted an elaborate wreath of variegated ivies and glittering red berries round the massive oaken newel at the head of the staircase; "but I should like Bruno to feel that it is Christmas-time directly he enters the Castle."

Lucille and her three assistants worked with good-will, from breakfast to a late luncheon; and among them they contrived to make the old hall, the wide shallow staircase, and long low corridor delightfully suggestive of Christmastide in the olden time. The polished oak panelling made such a good background, the many-coloured light from the painted window at the end of the corridor so helped and heightened the effect.

The Earl and Bruno, who were coming from the North that day, were not expected until dusk. It would be afternoon tea-time before they could arrive, the most delightful time at which to welcome them. Lucille's morning-room was glorious with hot-house flowers, bright with the soft red firelight, tempered by a ground-glass screen. The quaint little tables —Queen Anne, Japanese, Dundee—were daintily arranged by Lucille's own hands. Each low luxurious chair was in its most appropriate place; the fair young *châtelaine* herself in a dark-blue velvet gown, all slashed and puffed with deepest red, and with a red satin petticoat just peeping below the dark-blue drapery of the skirt. It was one of Lucille's trousseau gowns; and Tompion had told her that it was very unlucky to wear it—a tampering with futurity, which must result in something awful; but Lucille was bent upon looking her very best when Bruno and she met, after an agonising separation of nearly three weeks. The gown fitted her as never gown had fitted her before; and she stood in front of the cheval-glass innocently admiring herself.

"Well, Lady Lucille, it *do* give you a figure!" exclaimed Tompion; "but, for all that, I shouldn't like to wear it if I was you. I should feel I was flying in the face of Fate."

"I don't think Fate will take any notice of my new gown," said Lucille, pirouetting lightly, just to see the effect of the dark-blue stocking and the Queen Anne shoe. "And I want Bruno to be pleased. What is my finery meant for except to please him?"

"No, Lady Lucille, that's not it," protested Tompion, with a superior air. "Your trousseau is to do credit to your position as his lordship's only daughter. That's what you've got to study."

"I shall study nothing except my husband's happiness," answered Lucille; "and I hope that's what you mean to do, Tompion, when you are married."

Tompion breathed a despondent sigh.

"I never can bear to think of my marriage,"

she said; "for when I marry, you'll be having some stuck-up French maid who'll want you to paint your lips and pencil your eyebrows."

"No, she won't, Tompion; at least, she won't make such a suggestion a second time, I can assure you."

Tompion's marriage, which had been talked of for the last six years, had again been deferred unconditionally; and Lucille was to enter upon her new state encumbered with an old servant.

Lucille waited for the returning travellers alone in the winter gloaming, Miss Marjorum having discreetly gone to afternoon tea at the Vicarage. She sat a little way from the shaded hearth with an unheeded book in her lap, listening for the ring of wheels and horses' hoofs upon the frost-bound road. There it was at last; and then a sonorous peal at the big bell. Should she go to meet them? Had it been her father alone who was returning, she would have flown to the hall, and would have been in his arms before he could take off his overcoat. Had it been the Bruno of old days, she would have run to the head of the staircase to give him a laughing welcome. But a new sense of shyness restrained the betrothed bride. She waited by the fireside, with her heart beating fast and her colour coming and going, like the light and shadow on a rose that sways to and fro in the wind.

"Well, little lady, here you are at last!" said Lord Ingleshaw, as he and Bruno came into the firelight, bringing the frosty out-door atmosphere with them. "What a deathlike quiet there is in the house—almost like coming into a tomb!"

"Is that all the praise Lucille is to get for her Christmas decorations?" asked Bruno, when he and his betrothed had kissed, and she stood shyly at his side, hardly daring to look up at his face. "I thought the hall and staircase looked lovely."

"It all had a goblin air, to my mind," said the Earl, "such unearthly stillness."

"Dear father, you forget how quiet the Castle always is," said Lucille.

"Of course he does," exclaimed Bruno. "His lordship is demoralised by a great bustling hotel in a manufacturing city, where the waiters have as many different tongues as stopped the works at Babel, and where eager-looking Americans are always rushing in and out of the coffee-room. For my part, I am charmed to get back to the quiet of the fairy castle; and I should be content to be snow-bound here until—until my wedding-day."

He drew Lucille a little nearer to him as he spoke, the twilight favouring such gentle caresses.

He had come back to Ingleshaw determined to be
very happy, to value to the uttermost this treasure
of a pure and lovely woman's love which Providence
had given to him. What could he ever have better
in life than this perfect blessing, this constant in-
centive to good deeds and holy thoughts, this perpetual inspiration, this second conscience walking
at his side and guiding his steps, and always pointing upward?

"Come now, Lucille, you see before you the
member for the North-Eastern division of Smokeshire," said the Earl, laying his hand on Bruno's
shoulder. "How does he carry his dignity? Do
you think he has grown?"

"Miss Marjorum will be sure to say so," answered Lucille, laughing; "or, at any rate, she will
declare that he has expanded."

"His pockets have had to expand considerably,
I can assure you," said her father. "Now that
legislation has done its uttermost to insure the in-
corruptibility of electors, elections are just a little
more expensive than they were in the days of rank
rottenness. The voters are just as greedy, and they
are not half so candid."

"Have you ever observed anything of the professional beauty about me, Lucille?" asked Bruno.

"Well, not exactly."

"Yet I assure you there was as much eagerness to photograph me as if I had been the Lily herself. All the local photographers fell upon me like a pack of hounds. They told me it was customary for the member to be photographed; and it was furthermore customary for him to have his photograph enlarged by a twenty-guinea process, and provided with a handsome frame. The high-souled creatures would have scorned to accept a sixpence in the beaten way of bribery; but they all wanted to run me in for forty pounds' worth of photography. And this was only typical of the general sentiments."

"But why didn't you order the photographs?" asked Lucille naïvely. "I should have been enchanted to have them."

"What! six or seven enlarged me's? There are at least as many photographers in Billingford. No, I refused to yield to the charmers—first, because it would have been the encouragement of cool impudence; and secondly, because it would have been indirect bribery."

"But if you looked at things in such a Roman manner, and steadfastly refused to bribe, how was it you spent so much money?" asked Lucille, much puzzled.

"Ah, how indeed? You see, I had an agent."

"And he bribed for you?"

"He spent the money—on electioneering expenses. But now I am a member of the British Senate, and I am going to set about righting the wrongs of the universe. Is not that a great privilege?"

"I am very proud to think your talents will be of use in the world," said Lucille, seeing him, in the middle-distance of life, as Prime Minister. "But members of Parliament are never at home of an evening, are they?" she added regretfully.

"O, we must try to get the early-closing movement adopted at St. Stephen's. We ought, at any rate, to have our Wednesday evenings and our Saturday afternoons, like the counter-jumpers in small country towns."

A footman brought in lamps, while another brought the tea-tray; and Lucille's attention for the next five minutes was occupied with the delight of pouring out tea for the two people she loved best in the world. The shaded lamp gave only a subdued light, so she was not afraid of her happiness being too much in evidence. The sweet young face beamed with happy smiles; the soft blue eyes were luminous with delight.

"What a delicious thing in frocks!" said Bruno, sitting down close to her, on a capacious saddle-bag ottoman, and touching the velvet with the tips of his fingers. "Your Maidstone dressmaker is improving. There is a bold effect in those crimson slashings against dark blue which does credit to our county town."

"I am sorry to say this is not a Maidstone gown. It is Madame Muntzowski's."

"Indeed! Some other local genius! Sittingbourne, perhaps, or Sevenoaks?"

"Oh, Bruno! Madame Muntzowski is the new Polish dressmaker in Bruton-street."

"She may live in Park-lane for aught I care, so long as she preserves the knack of making you look so utterly lovely!"

Lord Ingleshaw had ensconced himself in the deepest and softest of the plush-covered armchairs. He had set down his empty cup already, and was half asleep, basking in the warmth and perfume, after a long cold railway journey. The lovers could talk what nonsense they pleased. Bruno had not felt so happy for ever so long as he felt this evening.

It seemed to him as if the old fresh sweet feelings had returned to him; those unspeakable feelings which had made the commencement of his courtship like a blissful dream. He had struggled with, and had overcome, that fatal fancy which had

so nearly wrecked his happiness. He had fought
against that strange and unhealthy fascination which
had made Elizabeth May's image a haunting thought
by day and night. He knew that he had been on
the threshold of hideous falsehood and wrong, and
he had recoiled horror-striken at the idea of his
own infamy.

Lord Ingleshaw slumbered for nearly an hour
in that comfortable plush-lined nest by the fire,
lulled by the low murmur of loving voices, as by the
sound of falling waters on a summer noontide.
Lucille and her lover could have talked to each
other for hours. He was full of his electioneering
experiences, of great plans for the future; measures
of all kinds for the enlightenment and happiness of
his fellow-men; measures which he was going to get
passed in the very teeth of prejudice and opposition,
fighting as St. George fought the dragon, as Macaulay
fought for Catholic Emancipation.

"How proud I shall be of your victories!" said
Lucille; "and I am sure that no one can stand up
against you. Eloquence like yours will overcome
everything."

"Ah, my dearest, it is so easy to talk by this
fireside, with one sweet sympathetic listener. I
shall seem a very different man to myself even at
Westminster, with some facetious member of the

Opposition crowing like a cock in the midst of my boldest flight of oratory, and my right arm working involuntarily like an automatic pump-handle."

"No one will crow while you are speaking," said Lucille, with conviction; "I know you are a heaven-born statesman, like William Pitt."

Miss Marjorum came in presently, and found Lord Ingleshaw snoring, and the lovers so deep in talk that they were unconscious of that nasal accompaniment to their conversation. The spinster's entrance dissolved the spell. His lordship started up and declared that he must dress for dinner, Bruno followed his example, and Lucille was left alone with her governess, who was brimming over with the last parish news. Lucille pretended to listen; but she was glad when Miss Marjorum went off to decorate herself for the evening, and left her alone with her happy thoughts. She sat down to the piano, and played her favourite bits of Mozart by memory. How those tender passionate airs, the "Vedrai carino," "Batti, batti," and "Voi che sapete," lent themselves to the reveries of love!

The little dinner of four was the gayest thing in dinners. The Earl, refreshed by a warm bath and a careful toilet, had recovered from the effects of his long cold journey. Bruno was in the highest spirits; he talked a great deal about his election,

and the humorous aspects of the free and inde-
pendent citizens of Smokeshire, and Lucille listened
with rapture.   In the evening they gave themselves
up to music, to the delight of Lord Ingleshaw, who
loved nothing better than to take his ease in his
armchair while his daughter sang or played to him.
There were some simple German duets, in which
Lucille's voice and her lover's harmonised deliciously
—verses all about love, and flowers, and stars, and
eventide.   Bruno had one of those sympathetic
baritone voices which are at their best in such
music, and Lucille's fresh young mezzo-soprano
sounded as untutored and free as the carolling of
a bird.

Lady Carlyon, who valued music merely as an
addition to a young woman's society charms, had
urged the necessity for lessons from an Italian
master, in order that a more brilliant and striking
effect might be obtained.

"When I was young all the girls sang 'Una voce.'
Why does not Lucille sing 'Una voce'?" she inquired;
"those little things of Mozart's are all very well before she is out; but in society I should like to hear
her do something better."

"In society I shall hold my tongue, auntie,"
Lucille answered, laughing. "People who can have

Patti or Nilsson at their parties won't want my little pipe."

"Not on state occasions, perhaps; but amateur concerts are very much in vogue, and I should like my niece to be able to distinguish herself. You ought to compose an occasional thing too—a gavotte, or a setting for one of Heine's ballads; it looks well."

This had been said before Lucille's engagement, but after her fate was settled the dowager became less exacting.

"You will have plenty of money, and you will be the future Countess of Ingleshaw," she said; "so you can do as you like. Very few girls jump into their independence so easily."

"Isn't it good of Bruno?" asked Lucille, smiling.

"Bruno could not have done better for himself," replied Lady Carlyon; he understands perfectly what is good for him."

This was one of those speeches that wound, like the feathery air-blown darts of a South American savage; so slight and light a thing, and yet so deadly. But now Lucille had forgotten her worldly-minded aunt's caustic speech and freezing philosophy. Bruno was restored to her, as tender and as true as he had been in the first days of their engagement.

Once in the course of the evening she found herself
wondering whether he had any curiosity about
Elizabeth May; whether he knew she was still
in the house, or concerned himself about her in any
way.

By one of those coincidences which seem like
magnetism, Lord Ingleshaw began to talk about
Elizabeth in the next moment.

"How is Lucille's *protégée?*" he asked, addressing
himself to Miss Marjorum, who sat by the fire knit-
ting a comforter. Miss Marjorum knitted comforters
for all the gaffers and goodies in the parish. "Still
grinding away at the three R's?"

"If you mean reading, writing, and arithmetic,
she conquered those three months ago. Rhetoric,
rhythm, and Roman history would answer better for
her present studies," replied Miss Marjorum proudly.
"All I can say is, I never had such a pupil—such
application, such tenacity of purpose, and such an
acute intelligence. I suppose the poor creature
feels that, for her, education is a matter of life or
death, just the one thing that can raise her out of
the Slough of Despond in which she was born and
bred."

"I am very glad to hear such a good account
of her," said the Earl. "I was rather afraid that
my daughter's imitation of the good Samaritan would

entail no end of trouble on all of us. You are not tired of your *protégée*, Lucille?"

"No, father, I am delighted to have been able to help—to help her to so good a friend as Miss Marjorum, that is to say," said Lucille, with a loving look at her old governess, "for it is to her careful teaching Elizabeth owes most. Mrs. Raymond is quite charmed with her, and has engaged her as nursery governess. I know she will be happy at the Dower House."

"No doubt of that," replied Lord Ingleshaw; "Mrs. Raymond is one of the best little women I know."

During this conversation Lucille's eyes had almost unconsciously watched Bruno's face. He sat in the full light of the lamp, turning over the leaves of a Doré Tennyson, as if in sheer emptiness of mind. His eyes were on the pictures as he slowly turned them over. If Elizabeth's name had power to quicken the beating of his heart, no quiver of brow or lip betrayed that influence. A marble image could not have been calmer than that broad open brow and that finely-moulded mouth. Yet this calmness cost Bruno Challoner no light effort. He had conquered the dangerous feeling which Elizabeth had aroused in him; but he had not forgotten her, and her memory was full of pain.

It was a relief, or it ought to have been a relief, to know that her future was comfortably provided for; that she would be sheltered in a home where her husband could scarcely venture to persecute her. There would, of course, always be the danger of his claiming her, so long as the marriage-tie remained unbroken; but it was probable that a man of that stamp would put himself out of court by leading an immoral life, and that the marriage might by and by be dissolved. All this was satisfactory, so far as Elizabeth was concerned; and it was undoubtedly a comfort to know that she had overcome any fatal *penchant*—betrayed so artlessly, yet with such impassioned looks, such thrilling tones, that night on board the yacht. Yes, all this was comfort, and knowing that it was so, Bruno wondered that his heart should wax heavy, his pulses throb tumultuously, at the very mention of this girl's name.

He closed the book suddenly, and looked up at Lucille. That sweet fair face was turned to him, the soft blue eyes seeking his with vague pathetic entreaty, as if she said, "Think of me, and of me only; lean on me; be true to me." "Yes, dear one," he answered, inwardly, "I will be true; I will hold fast by your love; and all will be well with us both in the end."

At eleven o'clock the butler brought in some old-fashioned spiced concoction of hot wine, which was supposed to have a peculiar appropriateness to Christmastide. The tankard that held it and the goblets into which it was poured were nearly three hundred years old—plate that had been buried under old Greek urns in the pleasaunce during the Civil War, and had thus escaped that period of general melting down. Lucille sipped a little of the mulled wine dutifully, not liking it at all, but accepting it as a libation to Father Christmas. Bruno did not scruple to make a wry face at the mixture, declaring that it was like a Mansion House loving-cup warmed up. And then they all drank happiness to each other, and peace and good-will to all men. Midnight was striking when Lucille and Miss Marjorum took their candles and retired. Lord Ingleshaw followed immediately, leaving Bruno to find his way to his rooms when he pleased. The young senator was in no hurry to retire. His brain was too highly strung for sleep to be possible yet awhile; so he raked the fading logs together, and sat in front of the low fire musing for nearly an hour before he rose slowly and meditatively, lighted his candle, extinguished the lamps, and went into the corridor.

All was dark outside. His solitary candle made

a faint spot of light upon the darkness of the long corridor, with its pictured faces, and old carved-oak cabinets projecting their bulky forms at intervals in the blank spaces between the doors.

"What a house for burglars!" thought Bruno. This after-midnight silence and darkness is apt to set people thinking of burglars, if they are happily exempt from the necessity of thinking about black-beetles. "Why, a dozen black-visaged gentlemen might hide behind those cabinets!"

Suddenly, at the farthest end of the long passage, a light shone out of the gloom, like a star. This, at an hour when the whole household was supposed to be hushed in sleep, was alarming. Did that distant light portend a ghost or a burglar?

Bruno advanced boldly to meet the unknown, afraid of neither phantom nor thief, but curious, and with his pulses stirred newly.

As he drew nearer to the figure he saw it was a woman, tall and slender, dressed in black. She was carrying a pile of books in one arm, a candle in the other hand; and she was that one woman whose presence had more power to agitate and disturb him than any ghostly visitant from the pale dust of dead and gone centuries.

He was not disloyal; he had fought a good fight: yet this woman could never be to him as other women; for in one fatal moment of their lives she had let him understand that she loved him, and was breaking her heart for love of him.

She did not hear his footstep on the thick Axminster carpet, and he was close to her when she looked up suddenly and saw him standing before her. She started and gave a little cry, while the topmost volume of the pile of books held against her breast slipped from her arms, and all the rest came down after it in a shower.

"I am so sorry," she faltered, kneeling to pick them up; "I hope the noise won't wake any one. I was going to take the books back to the library, in case his lordship should want them to morrow."

"I'll take them back for you," said Bruno kindly, and with a commonplace business-like tone which he felt to be worthy of much praise. "Is it not rather foolish to sit up reading till the small hours?"

"The time slipped by," answered Elizabeth meekly. "I am not a very good sleeper, so I like to get rid of some of the night. The winter nights are so dreadfully long."

Bruno remembered the time when no night was long enough for him; and the terrible conquest of inclination involved in getting up early, even for such delights as trout-fishing or cub-hunting. Of

late his nights had been not always unbroken by
long watches of troubled thought.

They were both kneeling, getting the scattered
volumes together by the light of the two candles on
the floor beside them. Bruno glanced at the titles
of the books. They were all poetry—the old-world
poets, in sober brown calf livery; a set which the
Earl loved and often looked at—Chaucer, Spenser,
Surrey, Wyatt, Waller, Herrick, Dryden.

"You have not read all these old fellows, have
you?" asked Bruno lightly.

"I only read bits here and there. It is so nice
to have a lot of books, and just to dip into one after
another."

"Yes, that is the luxury of reading. I don't suppose it is particularly good for one, any more than
a meal of ices and creams at a confectioner's; but
it is very nice."

The pleasant lightness of his tone would have
suited a conversation with some young lady in
society to whom he had just been introduced, and
of whom he knew nothing except that she was
there, and that he was expected to be civil to her.
Suddenly, as he rose with the pile of books in his
arms, he looked for the first time full in Elizabeth
May's face, and the revelation which flashed upon
him in that one look almost made him drop the

books as awkwardly as she had dropped them a few minutes ago.

That which he saw in the too brilliant eyes, the hectic bloom, the pale parted lips, was the stamp of death. Looking at her for a space which might be counted by moments, he saw enough to be terribly certain of her doom. This girl—rescued from fever-haunted alleys and crowded garrets, from dirt and disorder, squalor, horrors of every kind; sheltered and cared for, and surrounded with all the luxuries of refinement—had broken her heart, and was dying of rapid consumption. The fiery sword had worn out the scabbard.

What was it to him that she should so die? Nothing, perhaps; but he knew, he knew! Those vaguely-passionate broken sentences on board the yacht had told him too much. There are some for whom a first impassioned romantic love means triumph or death; and in this case triumph was impossible, and the girl must die.

He thought all this as he stood carefully re-adjusting the pile of slippery octavos, as if all his energies were absorbed in the one duty of conveying those books safely back to their shelf; and then, glancing at that wan face uneasily, he said,

"You are not looking so well as when I saw

you last. I'm afraid you must have been very ill since I left."

"O no," she answered lightly; "I am quite well. I have a rather troublesome cough, and I have bad nights; but there is nothing the matter with me. Mrs. Raymond is going to take me to Brighton at the beginning of the year, and then I shall get rid of my cough."

"Has Mr. Wharton seen you?"

"Yes; Lady Lucille insisted upon my seeing him. He gave me some stuff for my cough, and told me to wear warm clothes, and not to study so much. That was all."

"He is a fool!" said Bruno angrily. "I should like you— You ought to see a London physician —Jenner, Gull, Clark—somebody who has common sense."

"That would be a waste of money and trouble. I shall get quite well at Brighton," the girl answered with conviction.

Bruno was silent for a moment or so; and then, in a lowered voice, he asked,

"Have you heard any more of that man—your husband?"

"No, not a word. I am so thankful for that. I begin to hope that he is not coming here any more. Good-night, Mr. Challoner—if—if you are really going to be so kind as to take those books back to the library for me."

She made him a curtsy, just as she would have done to the Earl; and then went quickly to her room, the door of which was close by; leaving Bruno to carry the books down-stairs, through the dark silent house.

CHAPTER VIII.

AN OLD-FASHIONED CHRISTMAS.

"So are our gentle natures intertwined
With sweet humanities, and closely knit
In kindly sympathy with human kind."

CHRISTMAS-DAY passed very happily for Lucille, whose fair face was flushed with delight at having her lover at her side once more in the old square pew, where the crimson velvet cushions and foot-stools had faded almost to a neutral tint in the lapse of a century of Sundays, and where the most modern of the big quarto prayer-books contained a prayer for George and Charlotte, of pious domestic memory. It was a lovely clear frosty morning; not a black frost, by any means, but an ideal Christ-mas-day—warm in the sunlight, crisply cold in the shade; all the trees looking fairy-trees, and the lake crowded with village skaters in the early afternoon. Lucille and Bruno walked to and from church, calling on Mrs. Raymond at the Dower House on their way home.

The children here were full of inquiries about

Elizabeth, whom they called Miss May. They liked her so much, they told Bruno, who was a great favourite with them all. They were so glad she was going to be their governess. They meant to be very good, and learn all the lessons she set them; and then she would play hide-and-seek and Tom Tiddler with them—she had promised as much. And then they asked Bruno if he knew Tom Tiddler; to which Bruno replied that he had some recollection of having made the gentleman's acquaintance in very early days, before he went to Eton.

"But didn't you play at Tom Tiddler's ground at Eton?" inquired Totty, standing close up to Bruno's knee, with her eyes very wide open.

"No. We concentrated all our energies on cricket."

"Then what a nasty school Eton must be, if they wouldn't let you play Tom Tiddler!"

"Hard lines, wasn't it?" agreed Bruno; "a T. T. Club would have been a relaxation from the responsibilities of fielding and bowling."

"I like cricket," said Dotty, standing at Bruno's other knee, and speaking in a defiant voice.

"Then you oughtn't!" exclaimed Lotty; "it's a boys' game, and girls oughtn't to like boys' games!"

Mrs. Raymond at this juncture sent the children into the garden, lest they should become oppressive.

"You are too good to them, Mr. Challoner," she said; "and they are such talkative children; they have been allowed to say what they like, and they will express their opinions. Isn't it lucky they are so pleased with Miss May?"

"Yes, that is very fortunate," answered Bruno coolly, yet wondering all the while why the mere mention of Elizabeth's name should set his heart aching, just as a kindly-meant inquiry after chronic neuralgia will bring on the pain. "The very name of governess is enough to set some children against the person whom they are asked to receive in that capacity."

"O, but Miss May is so nice!" said Mrs. Raymond; "she has no governessish ways. Of course that is only natural, since this is to be her first attempt; but I find her positively charming. No one would imagine her a person of low antecedents; she is one of Nature's jewels."

"I'm afraid she is very ill," said Bruno, in a low serious voice. Lucille had been carried off to the garden by the children, to see their snow-man, a colossal figure of heaped-up snow, with a supposed semblance to humanity, carried out and accentuated by an inverted flower-pot, intended for a hat. "I saw her last night, by accident, and I was shocked by the change in her. She looks like a person who is going into a decline."

"O, no, no!" exclaimed Mrs. Raymond cheerfully, "I am sure there is nothing so serious as that. She has a winter cough, that's all. A fortnight of dear lively Brighton will set her up again."

"I don't think she ought to go to Brighton," said Bruno. "She ought to have the very best advice that London can give, and be sent off to the south of France without an hour's delay."

"And what is to become of Lotty, Dotty, and Totty?" cried Mrs. Raymond; "they are so fond of her."

"Lotty and Dotty can get another governess; but Elizabeth cannot get another life, if she throws away the one Providence has given her," answered Bruno, waxing stern.

"O Mr. Challoner, surely you cannot think me so selfish as to wish the dear girl to run any risk on my account!" protested Mrs. Raymond, with a grieved look. "I like her so much, and so do my children. If I thought there were anything serious I should be deeply concerned."

"I am sure she is seriously ill. I could not be mistaken in her appearance, though I saw her only for a few minutes. I don't want to alarm Lucille

—who—who is very sensitive, and very fond of her *protégée*. I know what a sensible practical woman you are, dear Mrs. Raymond, and I want you to take this poor creature in hand. Take her up to London to see a physician the very first day you can; go to the very best man you can—Jenner, I think. Money need be no consideration; I will send you a cheque. But don't let Lucille be made unhappy by knowing how very serious the case is."

"No, no, dear girl; so near her wedding too, when life is full of joy for her."

"Then I may rely upon your managing this for me?"

"Certainly. Let me see, we could not go to-morrow, Boxing-day—travelling would be impossible; and I suppose even the physicians take a holiday on that day. Shall we go the day after?"

"If you please. It might be best to write to Sir William Jenner by this evening's post, asking for an appointment."

"Yes, that shall be done."

They had just time for their talk when Lucille was brought back in triumph by the three chubby little girls, all in new gray velveteen frocks, point lace collars of motherly workmanship, and scarlet sashes. They had shown Lady Lucille all their treasures—snow-man, bantams, rabbits, and a goat which was being broken to harness, not without a tendency on his own part to breaking carriages.

"'Ady 'Ucille 'ikes my bunny best," cried Dotty, the youngest of these graces, who had not yet conquered the letter *l*.

"She says so 'cos you ast her, and she's too polite to say no," said Totty; "you didn't ought to have ast."

"'Ast' and 'didn't ought!'" cried Mrs. Raymond; "that is Phœbe's English. You see how badly we all want a governess."

"Mother doesn't!" exclaimed Lotty; "mother knows—O, such lots!"

"Be sure you are all with us before five," said Lucille, as she took leave of Mrs. Raymond.

There was to be a grand German Christmas-tree for the school-children at five o'clock, and a game at blind-man's buff afterwards for the little Raymonds and some other children of the genteel classes, in whom Lucille was interested.

Bruno felt more comfortable in his mind after that little talk with Mrs. Raymond. Elizabeth's face had haunted him, by fits and starts, all through the church service, coming back upon his mind every now and then, in his happier moments, like the memory of a great sorrow which will not let a man rest. He could not bear to think that she should

fade and perish before his eyes, and he make no
effort to save her. She was nothing, never could
be anything, to him; but she had loved him, and
for that fact alone she must always be sacred in
his thoughts.

Luncheon was almost as merry a meal as dinner
had been yesterday. The Vicar and his daughters
had been brought to the Castle by the Earl, and
they were full of life and spirits.

After luncheon they all walked down to the
lake to see the skaters; and Miss Marjorum created
some sensation by a new bonnet, which was in the
very latest Tunbridge Wells Parisian fashion, but
which was better adapted for exhibition in a
milliner's window—where one saw it only from an
abstract point of view—than on Miss Marjorum's
head.

"I didn't like to wear it in the morning," said
Miss Marjorum meekly, when the Vicarage girls had
complimented her. "I thought it might be too con-
spicuous for a village church."

"I'm afraid it would have distracted the school-
children," said Emma, the eldest girl.

"And it might have made them discontented
with their Dunstables," said Alice, the second.

Laura, the youngest, was hiding behind her sister,
speechless with laughter. That velvet monstrosity,

with its ostrich feather, fixed in its place by a
sprawling brass lizard, had been too much for her
equanimity.

Day was dying when they went back to the
Castle, with that pleasant darkness of early winter
evening—stars shining faintly in the dim gray sky,
a low streak of golden light slowly fading in the
far-off west. Lucille and Bruno walked side by side
through the leafless avenue, talking in low voices;
while the Vicarage girls skipped on in front of
them, prattling gaily with Miss Marjorum — the
youngest of the three was nine-and-twenty, but they
were spoken of everywhere as the Vicarage girls,
and will be so spoken of when the youngest is forty.
This was not flattery, but a friendly tribute to the
inherent girlishness and gushingness of the damsels, a perennial freshness which time could not
destroy.

The great hall of the Castle was brilliant with
the many-tapered Christmas-tree when they went in.
The logs in the wide stone fireplace burnt low, and
their red light was obscured by a broad Indian
screen, so as to concentrate the effect of those tiny
twinkling tapers, which shone upon every spray of
the tall yew-tree, one of the gardener's finest specimens, yielded up reluctantly for the occasion. Fairy-
like dolls were perched among the branches—dolls

in white and silvery raiment, with diadems on their
flaxen heads, and wands in their waxen hands;
angelic dolls, with golden wings; Watteau dolls,
with chintz frocks and beribboned crooks. Other
branches drooped heavily with baskets of sweet-
meats; cracker-bonbons hung in gorgeous festoons
from bough to bough; Tangerine oranges, tiny red
apples, showed bright amidst the sober green; gold
watches hung on every bough. Tompion and Elizabeth, with all the other maids to help them, had
been toiling since luncheon to produce this dazzling
effect. It was Elizabeth whose deft fingers had
dressed the dolls, and made the seraphic wings
and fairy wands out of gilt paper. It had pleased
her to be thus useful, even with that gnawing pain
in her side all the time she worked—that ever-
increasing languor which made work so difficult.

As if this marvellous tree—this lovely invention
from that land of elves and goblins somewhere
under the shadow of the Harz Mountains—were
not enough, there was a wonderful institution called
a "bran-pie," in a dusky corner of the hall; and
into this bran-pie every little hand was to be dipped, to catch what it could amidst the mystery of
bran.

The children, gentle and simple, were all flock-
ing into the hall as Bruno and Lucille and the

Vicarage girls came in from their walk. Time had flown so swiftly for Lucille.

"Is it really five?" she exclaimed, astonished. "I never heard it strike four."

"It's ever so much past five," cried Totty; "and you told us to come at five. We've been waiting ages."

"Totty, what a rude child you are!" exclaimed Mrs. Raymond.

Totty ran to Lucille with the basket full of tickets.

"Please, mayn't we begin to draw?" she asked.

"But when you have all drawn you'll want to pull the tree to pieces," said Lucille.

"No, I won't; but I should like to be able to look at a doll, and know that it is mine," answered Totty.

Lots were drawn, and a tall footman unhooked all the dolls and watches and bonbon-baskets, which were most accurately distributed, leaving the tree still glorious with its innumerable tapers and festoons of gold and silver. The treasures were shared indiscriminately by gentle and simple. There were no galling distinctions: only Lotty, who was known to be a clever child, was seen to absorb a good many toys by a system of exchange and barter, and by taking toys bodily from stupid open-mouthed infants who had not been educated up to their acquisitions, and relinquished them to any sturdy assailant in sheer helplessness.

Bruno caught a glimpse of Elizabeth May in the distance, among the upper servants, looking flushed, and radiant with an unearthly brightness. She wore some scarlet ribbon about her neck, and a gold locket which Lady Lucille had given her that morning as a Christmas present; and her new black gown fitted her so well as to accentuate her alarming slimness. She looked a mere reed, and a reed that could be easily snapped in twain.

Mrs. Raymond, alarmed by Bruno, took occasion to observe her more closely than she had done hitherto, and she, too, saw good ground for apprehension. But she was careful not to scare the patient.

"I don't like that nasty little worrying cough of yours, Miss May," she said lightly. "I think I shall take you to London the day after to-morrow to see some kind clever doctor, who will set you all right again before we go to Brighton."

"I don't think it's worth while," answered Elizabeth. "You are all of you too kind to me. I daresay my cough will go of its own accord when the summer comes."

"No doubt; but that is rather too long to wait.

A clever doctor will get rid of it much sooner. Good gracious, what *is* Dotty doing?"

Dotty, the youngest of the three chubby daughters, was fighting the eldest of the Vicarage girls over the ruins of the bran-pie, which Dotty, in her eagerness to explore its inmost treasures, had turned upside-down. And now she wanted to have her pick of the scattered contents, an act of marauding which the Vicarage girl would not allow.

"No, no, Dotty; the school-children must have their share," protested Emma. Whereupon Dotty attacked her with clenched fists—chubby pink paws rolled up into tight little balls of flesh—pummelling her adversary's waistband.

"O, you dreadful child!" cried Mrs. Raymond, snatching up the spoilt darling. "The Christmas-tree has quite turned her head."

"I want more toys!" shrieked Dotty, in baby accents; and was led away by Elizabeth, still shrieking, to be restored to composure, and to return, ten minutes afterwards, with washed face, a meek and lamblike image of childhood, to take her place at the tea-table in the long dining-room, where the simple children were entertained at two long tables, and the gentle children at a shorter table placed across the upper end of the room.

Mrs. Raymond, Tompion, and Elizabeth waited

on Lucille and the three Vicarage girls, whose pleasing duty it was to go on pouring out tea without intermission for the next hour. When the children had stuffed themselves with cake and buns and bread-and-jam, liquefying that stodgy mixture with warm tea, the tables were cleared and rearranged for the mothers and aunts and elder sisters, who all came to this afternoon entertainment, and for whom there was a second bran-pie, containing ribbons and gloves and Prayer-books and hymn-books and *Christian Years*. The men were to have a great supper of beef and pudding in the hall at nine o'clock, when the Christmas-tree was dead and gone, the tapers all burnt out, and the ill-used yew restored to the anxious gardener, to be nursed into health and vigour after this frightful shock to his constitution.

The children were playing at blind-man's buff in the hall while the matrons and maids were at tea. The joyous ring of their voices went echoing among the rafters in the fine old Gothic roof. Lucille and Bruno and the Vicarage girls left the older party to the care of Mrs. Raymond and Elizabeth May, and went to have half an hour's romp with the little ones before the warning gong should sound at half-past seven and disperse the assembly. Lucille's face was lovely in the soft light of the tapers as she and Bruno drew near the Christmas-tree. There was no other light in the hall, except the glow of the wood fire and an occasional sparkle of flame, as one log, slowly crumbling to ruin, reeled over and struck against the others, spluttering sparks as it fell.

"My love, how sweet you look!" said Bruno, touched by the tender light in Lucille's soft eyes. "This is the kind of party which sets you off to the best advantage. I doubt if you would look half so lovely if you were entertaining the county."

"It is so nice to make these little things happy," answered Lucille quietly. "They have so few pleasures! Why, do you know, they begin to look forward to their Christmas-treat directly the summer school-feast is over! But this year we are giving them a grander entertainment than usual. My dear father wished it to be so, in honour of—"

"Of our approaching marriage. How proud I ought to feel!" said Bruno. "Next year I shall have a hand in the preparations. We will do something out of the common. What should you say to a mystery play—Saul and the Witch of Endor, or Daniel in the Den of Lions? I feel that it is in me to make a great effect as a witch or a lion."

"I should not like to make light of sacred

things," remonstrated Lucille gently. She had been educated in a somewhat old-fashioned reverence for the Bible.

"O, but the grand old picturesque stories, we may make what use we please of those, I think," said Bruno. "The bishops treat them very lightly in the Speaker's Commentary. They manage to account for everything in a pleasant rational way. I daresay they explain the civility of Daniel's lions by supposing that they were the worn-out veterans of the royal Zoo, toothless and overfed."

Lucille looked quite unhappy at this horrible suggestion; and just then an avalanche of children, all rushing away from an ubiquitous blind-man, in the person of the youngest Vicarage girl, swept against the lovers, and entangled them in the game. The Vicarage girl, who seemed to be all eyes, pounced on Bruno; whereupon he had to be blind-folded, and went about catching children in arm-fuls of half a dozen at a time, after the manner of an ogre who wanted to spit them like larks, or bake them in a pie, with their toes sticking up out of the pastry.

The game proceeded with riotous mirth, till the sound of the great gong rose booming and buzzing through the hall, like some gigantic bumble-bee which had lost his way, and was knocking his head against the painted windows.

"Now then, all you little Cinderellas," cried Bruno, throwing off his bandage, "scurry home before your glass slippers fall off, for we have no princes for husbands in this country!"

The mothers and aunts came in from the tea-room, and swept up their belongings. Comforters and hats were put on, gratitude for the treat was expressed in pleasant rustic accents, curtsies were made to the donors of the feast, and then away they all went, gentle and simple, tripping briskly over the frost-bound paths, while Lucille ran to her dressing-room to put on her dinner-gown.

There was to be no one but the family at dinner. Lord Ingleshaw had been dozing over his favourite Variorum Horace all the afternoon, hearing the clamour of childish voices and the prancing of little feet afar off, subdued by thick doors and tapestry curtains. When the children were gone he emerged from his retirement, and looked at the Christmas-tree, with its tapers waxing low, like so many lives fading out, and heard, with satisfaction, that his daughter's festival had been a great success. He found Elizabeth May in the hall, extinguishing the tapers and stripping the tree of its tinsel decorations.

"What an industrious young woman you are, Elizabeth!" he said kindly; "I hear that the greater part of this tree was your work."

"It was a great pleasure to work for it. I never saw a Christmas-tree before, my lord; I never went to church on a Christmas-day before; I never knew what Christmas meant till Lady Lucille taught me. O, how happy and good it all is, and how different from the life in the alley where I used to live! I wish some one would do something for those poor children at Christmas."

"Surely some one does. There are good people all over London trying to help," said Lord Ingleshaw.

"Yes, I know there is a great deal done; but there are so many who want help. There are so many dreadful holes and corners that ought to be done away with altogether; yet, if they were pulled down, where could the poor creatures go? There is a new city wanted in London—a city built for the poor, and owned by the rich. Poor landlords and poor tenants—that means misery."

"And by a rich landlord I suppose you mean a man who doesn't expect to get any rent?" said his lordship.

"No, my lord; only a man who will give fair

value for the money—a man who will see that his tenants drink pure water, and are not poisoned in their wretched houses. Let him be as exacting as he likes to get his due, but let him give us our due, and not take advantage of our helplessness. We must live near our work, whatever it is. The landlords know that, and they won't spent a shilling upon the fever-dens that are always crowded—yes, even when death is the tenant one hears of oftenest."

"There are the Peabody houses."

"Not half enough of them. We want more, and on a humbler scale. My heart aches when I think of what I have seen the little children and the old people suffer. Those who can go out and work are better off; but those that have to stay at home, and huddle together in those wretched rooms, and breathe that poisoned air—O, my lord, how hard it is for them! I was ill once, and lay in my attic for weeks, and I know what it was."

"Poor creatures!" sighed his lordship. "It is a hard nut for legislators and philanthropists to crack. We must get Mr. Challoner to take up the question next session. Well, Elizabeth, I am glad to see you happy and useful. Everybody speaks well of you. And that husband of yours—you have heard no more of him?"

"No, my lord, thank God!"

"So say I. We will do our best to protect you from him, come when he may."

———

CHAPTER IX.

FAITHFUL UNTO DEATH.

"Some innocents 'scape not the thunderbolt."

IT was about ten minutes before nine, and the men and lads were coming lumbering into the great hall, looking just a little clumsier than usual in their Sunday raiment—a good deal of it new, in honour of Christmas; for it is well that such an important event as a new coat and waistcoat should be marked and, as it were, sanctified by some great day in the calendar, being so much easier for reference as an unmistakable date ever afterwards. Gaffer Goodlake would never forget that he wore his olive-green coat with brass buttons for the first time on Christmas-day. The sound of joy-bells would be associated with that garment for ever after; even when it came to be an every-day coat; going forth to its labour in the dewy mornings, and coming home dusty in the shadowy evenings; sitting under flowery hedges in the sunny noontide, and lying down for a brief snatch of slumber among the foxgloves and ragged-robins after the labourer's frugal meal.

Lord Ingleshaw and his family were dining in a pretty room on the upper floor opening into the long corridor, a good way from the hall, but on a level with the musicians' gallery, where all those servants who were not actually employed had assembled to watch the village-feast. The housekeeper was there, in her purple brocade gown—a gown bought in a long-ago period, when every well-to-do matron had her brocade gown—and which Fashion's revolving wheel had made again the mode.

"I never thought I should live to see brocades come in again," said Mrs. Prince, as she put on her purple garment, "after the run there was upon morees; but so long as I've got a silk that can stand on end for richness, I don't care two straws for the fashion."

"That's not *my* way," said Tompion; "I'd rather have a gingham made in the last fashion than silk-velvet if it was out of date. Give me style."

Mrs. Prince, Tompion, Elizabeth, and all the housemaids had assembled in the gallery. In a separate group were the old man-cook—whose *cuisine* dated from the time of the Reform Bill, and who had lived at the Castle so long, and had so little work, that he had almost forgotten even that antique school of cookery—the clerk of the kitchen, and a butler or two. Dinner was finished in the Wouvermans room, and the family were dawdling over dessert, so the butlers were off duty. The village supper had been cooked by the kitchen-maid, and was being served by underlings. The upper servants looked on at the festivities of the lower classes as at a play.

"There's old father," said one of the house-maids, pointing out her parent to her companion, as he shuffled into his place at the board. "I hope he'll behave. He does put his knife into his mouth dreadful. I never care to sit down to a meal at home, though they're ever so pressing. When one is used to having everything set before one nicely it makes such a difference."

The chief gardener sat at the head of the table, and carved. He was a Kentish man born and bred; and though he felt he had left these rustics far behind in the march of civilisation, to say no-thing of having saved a good bit of money, there was a bond between them. They had picked hops together on crisp October mornings years ago, when he was one of many cottage-children, poorly fed and clad, bringing his meagre little handful of grist to the family mill. He had worked hard and learned hard, and had made the very most of his intelligence in an intelligent form of industry; while these other poor fellows had laboured with their hands, and legs, and loins alone, digging, and delving, and bush-harrowing, and ditching, and never rising above the rudest form of labour. He looked down upon them kindly from his lofty height, and smiled on them benignantly, as he sliced the savoury baron of beef, and filled plate after plate with that substantial fare.

Elizabeth May looked down at the cheerful scene—the long tables spread with that fine old pewter dinner-service which was one of the glories of Ingleshaw, the big brown beer-jugs, the bonny home-made loaves on broad wooden platters, the huge Cheshire cheese at one end of the table, a look of almost Gargantuan plenty on the board. Mrs. Prince had taken Elizabeth into particular favour, and, sheltered by that ponderous matron, she stood quite apart from Tompion and the rest of the maids, who were sniggering together, with their elbows resting on the gallery-rails, at the uncouth ways of their kinsfolk below. Some of them had sweethearts in that rural assembly, and were interested in watching the vigorous manner in which those favoured ones despatched their beef and beer.

Elizabeth watched the scene with only a faint interest. She had been pleased and amused by the little children, with their fresh rosy cheeks and starry eyes; but these dull clodhoppers, with their

gruff voices and loud laughter, their boorish movements and gigantic appetites, were hardly a pleasing sight. The old men, perhaps, were the most
interesting; there was mute pathos in those bent
shoulders, bowed with the labour of long years,
that silvery hair worn of a patriarchal length. Were
Abraham and Isaac and Jacob old men like that,
Elizabeth wondered, bent and worn with field labour,
fulfilling in the most literal manner God's curse
upon man's disobedience? or were they grander
figures, masters of many servants, owners of flocks
and herds, lording it over their slaves, and eating
the fat of the land? That story of Isaac's death-
bed had always brought before her mind the picture of an old field-labourer, bent, and haggard,
and worn with toil, eating his last meal with
poverty's keen hunger, and leaving a heritage of
homely labour to his sons.

Gradually, as she looked down at the lighted
hall, she grew to distinguish the various figures, to
identify and individualise different faces in the four
long rows of revellers. There was one man, near
the upper end of the table, whose appearance
puzzled her. He was so different in look and movements from the others. She was sure that he was
a stranger, for she saw that no one spoke to him,
and that, although he tried now and then to join in

the conversation at his end of the table, the attempt
always fell through, and he remained outside the
circle, looking on with eager crafty eyes.

This man was a Londoner, Elizabeth felt assured.   There was an indefinable something in his
every movement which belonged to the costermonger
class—the men born and bred in London alleys,
steeped to the lips in a city life.   That ferret-like
eye, that peculiar cut of the jaw, so intensely expressive of cunning, were never seen in a field-
labourer.   Those sidelong glances and bird-like mo-
tions of the head—the movements of a creature
that is always on the watch, the movements of a
bird of prey—she had seen them all among her old
acquaintance, and she had never seen the same
type among the Kentish villagers.

There was no reason that a London labourer
should not, by some chance, find himself fairly en-
titled to a Christmas-supper at Lord Ingleshaw's
expense.   Yet the presence of this man disturbed
Elizabeth, and she would have been very glad to
discover how he came there.

"Do you know who that man is—the man with
the long red hair, the fourth from the upper end of
the table?" she asked Mrs. Prince.

"Lor', no, my dear," answered the housekeeper;
"I don't know half of them at this distance, not

even with my specs, and as to pointing out any one
of 'em, I couldn't do it. But it's a very pretty sight,
isn't it? And doesn't our fine old pewter service
look lovely?"

Elizabeth could hardly take her eyes from the
man with the long red hair—a regular shock of
coarse rough hair, very different from the close
horsey cut usually affected by the London coster;
and yet she was not the less certain, despite a very
elaborate smock-frock, that this man was a Londoner, so vividly did his appearance recall the as-
sociates of her early days.

Supper was finished in about three-quarters of
an hour, and then came a good half-hour for
speeches and songs. The speeches were short, but
the songs were long and of a narrative kind, with
choruses which, in some cases, seemed slightly irre-
levant, not to say unintelligible, but which were
executed with much spirit, and gave general satisfaction. As the joviality of the company increased,
under the inspiring influence of music, Elizabeth
saw that the red-haired man had made for himself
a friend in the person of an under-gardener who
sat next him, and with whom he was now in close
conversation—so close that neither of the two joined
in the chorus of the song now going forward.

Elizabeth knew this under-gardener for an hon-

est simple-minded youth, a picture of grinning good-
nature, a lad who would be ready to make friends
with anybody.

At half-past ten the entertainment was all over,
and the men were dispersing. Just as they were
clearing out of the hall—the red-haired man and
James Morley, the gardener, still hanging together
—Elizabeth's attention was distracted by Mrs. Prince.

"We're going to have a bit of hot supper in my
room," she said—"Mr. Scrimger, Jones, and Mason,
and Tompion, and Mary Milford. You might as
well join us, Miss May, if you're not above sitting
down with servants now that you're going to be a
governess. It'll be your first and last Christmas at
Ingleshaw Castle, I suppose."

"Indeed, I don't hold myself above anybody in
this house," said Elizabeth eagerly; "I hope no one
will ever think that. I know how low I am, and
that I was brought here out of charity. I shall
never forget that. But you must excuse me to-night,
dear Mrs. Prince; I have a bad headache, and I
couldn't eat any supper."

"Poor thing! You worked too hard at that Christmas-tree all the afternoon," said the housekeeper
compassionately. "I never knew such a girl to
work; I only wish the others were like you. Well,
you shall go to your room, and I'll bring you a

glass of hot negus the last thing, or a little egg-flip."

"No, indeed, I couldn't take any."

"O, but you must; I'll bring it as I go up to bed. Come, Tompion!"

They all trooped down-stairs, leaving Elizabeth alone in the gallery. She sank down into a chair in a corner, very glad to be alone. Her side was aching, and her heart ached too, though she hardly knew why. God had been very good to her. She had come to Ingleshaw Castle a beggar in rags, newly released from the sick-ward of one workhouse, and with no better prospect than the casual-ward of another workhouse. She had been brought to this beautiful home, and had been purified from the taint of her old life, and fed, and clothed, and taught, and transformed into a new creature. And now she stood on the threshold of a new life, a useful life, in which her own labour should pay the cost of her maintenance. No one could reproach her as a beggar, or a hanger-on upon the skirts of charity, when she was Mrs. Raymond's governess. And yet the thought of that new life brought her no ray of hope. It seemed to her that she was going to be parted for ever from all that made life worth having, when she had seen the last of Bruno Challoner. To be near him, to be a servant—yes, even the lowest scullion—in the house to which he came, or in which he lived, would be a life not altogether unblessed; but to exist in the outer darkness of a world upon which he never entered—O, how blank and dreary the prospect of such an existence seemed to her!

She looked back, as she sat listless, supine, in her corner, leaning against the massive oaken balustrade, the great empty hall, lit only by the low glimmer of dying logs, lying below her like a dark gulf. She looked back, and remembered those summer days in which she had been the messenger between Lady Lucille and her lover; when she had seen and talked with Bruno Challoner ever so many times in the day, comforting him when he was downcast, bringing him tender messages from his betrothed, answering the same anxious questions again and again as they two strolled up and down the grassy space below Lady Lucille's windows.

She remembered how gracious he had been to her; how grateful for the comfort she had carried to him; how he had seemed to give her the credit of every cheering report; with what exquisite tenderness he had spoken of the sick girl lying in her darkened room up yonder, behind the silken curtains. And then she remembered how as the slow summer days went by she began to look forward to those meetings in the rose-garden with a strange delight, longing for the hour that brought Bruno Challoner to her side, dwelling upon his words, keeping his looks and tones locked in her heart; haunted by his face all the time they were parted, thrilled by the sight of him when they met, as if that face were something new and strange. He was so different from—so far above—all the men she had known in her past life. The refinement of his manner, his graciousness, the music of his voice, his lofty bearing, made him seem a godlike creature in the sight of her who had been familiar only with the outcasts of this earth, the refuse of humanity. This was her sole excuse for loving him. But she did not sin deliberately. The fatal passion crept into her heart unawares.

Then came the long days of Lady Lucille's convalescence, during which Mr. Challoner was altogether absent; and then that August morning on the sands at Weymouth, when the lovers met after their enforced separation, and Elizabeth, not yet schooled in self-governance, rebelled against Fate as she paced the bay, alone and forgotten, while those two sat side by side, a little way off, all the world to each other. And then followed days of delight on board the yacht—days when she made a third in all their talk, lived with them and be-

longed to them—days in which Bruno seemed almost as much to her as he was to his plighted wife.
A time of false unholy happiness—delusive, ensnar-
ing—which ended that September night, when, in a
moment of reckless, headlong, half-despairing passion,
she betrayed her fatal secret, and let Bruno Challoner into the secret of his own weakness, which
had made this nameless waif for a little while dearer
to him than his betrothed. He had fought, and
fought manfully, against his folly, and from that
hour all familiar every-day association between him
and Elizabeth, as between friends and equals, ceased
for ever. She hated herself for the madness of that
moment, the uncontrollable impulse which had wrung
the truth from her despairing soul; and the thought
that he scorned her for that folly galled her proud
spirit, and made the burden of life almost unbear-
able. Then it was that the sword began to prey
too fiercely on the scabbard, and that the very
foundations of life were sapped. She, who had out-
lived hunger, cold, fever and squalor, privations and
hardships unspeakable, succumbed to the more bitter
agony of a bruised and broken spirit.

There was comfort for the wounded soul in
that brief interview in the wood, when Bruno told
her to be brave, and revealed his own weakness;
there was comfort in the knowledge that he had

never scorned her. He, whose voice trembled as he spoke to her, whose hand clasped hers in such intensity of hopeless passion, could never have despised her.

She would be brave for his sake, true for his sake; she would die sooner than that Lady Lucille should ever know that either of them had been false. Her thoughts went slowly back over that passionate, sorrowful past, as she sat in the dark gallery, lighted only by the lamp in the corridor—light that came faintly through a half-open door. Looking back to-night, life seemed strange and dreamlike; it was as if she were recalling some-body else's story rather than her own. She seemed to have passed beyond caring very much about anything. Grief had lost the sharpness of its sting. The pain was dull and deadened, but the future was quite hopeless. It was as if she stood on some little island—a mere rock—in the midst of the wide desolate sea, not caring to look to one side or the other, where all the prospect was blank and joyless.

She was glad to think she would be far away, at some unknown place by the sea, when Mr. Challoner and Lady Lucille were married. She could have schooled herself to look on at the wedding calmly enough, having acquired a wonderful

power of self-command during the last three months;
but still she would have felt somehow like a skeleton
at the feast.   She could not have rejoiced as others
rejoiced, with honest unfaltering heart.   Only yesterday, when Lady Lucille called her into her dressing-
room to see the white satin wedding-gown, out-
spread upon a sofa in all its glistening loveliness,
half veiled in softest lace, and garlanded with orange-
blossoms, she had shrunk shudderingly away, fancy-
ing that she saw a shroud lying there.

"It will be your turn to be married soon, I daresay," said Lucille, knowing nothing about Tom
Brook, "and then I shall give you your wedding-
gown."

The clock struck eleven.   Sounds of music, or
of laughter, came now and then from the corridor.
The little Christmas party were sitting in Lucille's
morning-room, just as they had sat last night.   It
was one of the prettiest rooms in the Castle, and
the Earl preferred it to any, except his library.
Once the door remained open all through "Batti,
batti," which Lucille sang exquisitely.   O, what
tenderness, what deep love, the melody breathed
from those young lips! Elizabeth could guess how
Bruno stood by the piano, looking down at her as
she sang; or sat close by the angle of the instru-

ment, with his face on a level with the singer's.
So she would sing to him for many and many a
year to come, till Time dulled the freshness of the
voice; but it would be sweet in his ears to the end,
sweetest when he heard her singing to her children.
No one could doubt that those two would be happy
together, for they loved each other with a deep-
rooted affection, a love of old days and early years,
which no fleeting passion, born of a truant fancy,
could undermine.

While Elizabeth sat in her corner of the shadowy
gallery there were warmth and life and brightness
in Lady Lucille's morning-room, from which the
sound of music and voice came with such pathetic
meaning to the ear of that lonely listener. Never
had Lucille felt happier than she felt to-night,
never more secure of her lover's affection. The
cloud that had been between them for a little
while had passed away altogether, and perfect confidence was restored. Lord Ingleshaw looked on
from his easy-chair by the hearth, as those two sat
by the piano—looked on with silent rejoicing, grateful to Providence, which, in this union, had fulfilled
his long-cherished desire. He had never told
Lucille how fondly he hoped for her marriage with
his heir; how dear a dream it had ever been with
him to picture his daughter in the old home, her

husband occupying that place which his son would
have held had his wife lived to give him a son.
Not for worlds would he have influenced her choice,
in order to gratify any desire of his. He loved her
too well for that. But this thing had come about
naturally, without his interference, and he was
deeply thankful. God had been very good to him.

"My little Lucille," he said presently, when his
daughter crept to his side, and knelt down by the
arm of his chair, and nestled her fair head against
his shoulder, "my dear one, it seems only yesterday
that you were a child upon my knees. And now
so soon to be a wife! I used to think the years
were long and slow! but now I know how swift my
darling has made them for me. I can measure the
tranquillity of my days by your growth, Lucille.
You have grown from a baby to a woman almost
unawares."

"It has seemed a long, long life to me, dear
father," said Lucille, "but not an hour too long.
You dream away so many hours over Horace and
Virgil, and all your favourite books, that I daresay
the days do slip by unawares."

"True," said the Earl, "I waste a good deal of
time among my books: but it is pleasant dreaming.
And I mean to be more active in future. I shall
help Bruno in all his humanitarian schemes. Eli-

zabeth May has been talking to me about the
dwellings of the London poor—that is a subject I
should like to go into thoroughly. But it is too
late to talk about it to-night. There goes half-past
eleven, a most unholy hour for Ingleshaw Castle.
Suppose you read us Milton's hymn, Lucille, to give
us a comfortable Christmastide feeling before we
go to bed. You used to read those noble verses
very prettily."

"I taught her," said Miss Marjorum, folding her
mittened hands, and smiling the smile of self-satis-
faction. "Before she was twelve years old I had
made her familiar with some of the masterpieces
of our language. She knows the 'Hymn to the
Nativity' by heart."

Lucille, sitting on a stool by her father's chair,
sheltered from observation, began, in her calm,
well-modulated voice, the grand Miltonic hymn,

> "It was the winter wild
>   While the heaven-born Child
>   All meanly wrapt in the rude manger."

Miss Marjorum was not a genius, but she was a
most capable teacher, and she had taught her pupil
to pronounce her own language, a gift which very
few young ladies of the present day possess, or
perhaps would care to possess; for there is a savour
of the archaic in the English tongue so spoken, as

old-fashioned as the prose of Addison. Young
ladies prefer, for the most part, to talk society
language, which is almost as unlike English as if
it were Ojibbeway, and which tortures and mys-
tifies the intelligent foreigner who has learnt our
language out of books.

Lucille recited without bombast or rant of any
kind—calmly, quietly, but with a clear and finished
utterance, and with the expression which results
naturally from perfect intelligence.

Bruno listened with delight. It was a new gift
revealed to him in his future wife.

"It is better than music. You shall recite for
me every evening when we are alone, Lucille," he
said, with serio-comic authority. "You can get up
your Milton and your Keats, your Wordsworth and
your Shelley, in the odd half-hours of your day;
and after dinner, when I am worn-out with public
work, you can recite to me, as I lie on the sofa and
smoke. It will soothe my harassed nerves."

And now, on the stroke of twelve, they bade
each other good-night, after a Christmas-day without a cloud. Few such happy days come into any
lifetime; days at once good and happy, since they
have ministered to the happiness of the many.

Midnight sounded from the clock in the Gothic

gateway, from the clock in the stables, from the old
eight-day clock on the staircase, and the Louis
Quatorze bracket-clock in the corridor. All was
hushed and dark in the Castle; but still Elizabeth
sat in her corner of the gallery, with no more inclination for sleep than if it had been midday instead of midnight. She had watched the servants
in the hall below—two of them going their rounds
with a lantern, locking and bolting doors, and making sure that all was secure for the night. They
performed their work in a somewhat perfunctory
manner on this occasion, as men who had supped
heavily off the lukewarm remains of the "baron,"
and who had not been limited in the item of beer.
A dozen burglars might have hidden in the Gothic
hall while the two men went round with their
lantern, peering into the corner to which its rays
were directed, and ignoring all the rest of the hall.
The figures in armour, behind which it would be
so easy for a living man to conceal himself; the
big oaken settles; the tall Japanese screen, which
fenced off the draught from one door; the heavy
tapestry curtain hanging before another—all these
remained unexplored by men or by lantern. There
was infinite security to the minds of the two cus-
todians in the very sound of the ponderous bolts, in the
very scroop of the mighty keys in the ancient locks.

16*

When they were gone, Elizabeth looked over into the hall from her corner, which was in deepest shadow. The moon had risen, and her cold clear light streamed through the high painted window in the wall behind Elizabeth, and flooded that side of the hall opposite to her hiding-place. The plated armour sent forth silvery gleams in that romantic light. A little while ago, before the men came to lock the doors, Elizabeth had fancied she saw one of those effigies of dead and gone warriors faintly stirred, as if some one had moved behind it. This was nearly an hour ago, by the red light of the expiring fire. Now, by the more vivid light of the moon, she distinctly saw one of those armour-men shiver upon his base, and a dark figure stirring behind it. Then the living figure crept out from behind the armed image, and moved stealthily towards the curtained doorway which opened into an anteroom communicating with the Earl's library. She saw him lift the curtain, and go into the anteroom, and then, in the absolute stillness of the house, she heard the opening of a window and the gruff murmur of men's voices. There were midnight intruders in the Castle—secret intruders, who must needs mean evil.

What should she do—alarm the house, and get those men taken into custody? They had not seen her. She could easily slip away by the corridor to the back staircase and the tower in which the men-servants slept, and the household would rise, strong in numbers, capable of defying a band of burglars, be they never so desperate. One consideration only restrained Elizabeth from hastening, as far as her feet would carry her, to the house-steward's door. She had the face of that red-haired man still in her mind. She had been recalling it, puzzling herself about it, trying desperately to make it out, since the revellers dispersed; and she knew now that the savage projecting jaw, the thin lips, the crafty look, belonged to her husband, Tom Brook, and no other. She remembered her fears after that meeting in October, how closely Tom Brook had questioned her about the interior of the Castle—questions from which she had withheld all satisfactory replies. And now she felt very sure that Brook had entered the Castle, disguised and unsuspected, among the crowd of villagers. To give the alarm would be to destroy the man who had once cared for her and cherished her, after his brutal fashion. Yet she was resolutely bent upon hindering Tom Brook and his accomplices from doing any wrong to life or property in that house.

She knew that the plate-room was on the same level as the library, at the end of a narrow passage

behind that apartment. She knew that it was pro-
tected by an iron door, which would not be easily
violated. She had heard of the perfection to which
the art of burglary had been brought of late years,
and she knew that it was possible for the skill of a
highly-trained thief to set locks and iron doors at
defiance; but she knew that this could not be done
quickly. There was time for deliberation on her
part before she interfered to protect her benefactor's
property.

She slipped off her shoes, and crept softly down
the broad oak staircase, and across the wide moonlit
hall, to that curtained doorway, dreading lest she
should be seen by some one watching on the
threshold of the anteroom. But there was no such
watcher. She lifted the tapestry, and crept into the
anteroom. There was no light except the light of
the winter sky reflected upon the snowy whiteness
below—a cold ghastly glare, which gave all things
an unearthly look. The shutters were unfastened,
and one lattice of the mullioned window stood wide
open. The wintry air blew in upon her, chilling
her to the heart. She had no doubt that this window
had been opened by Tom Brook a few minutes ago,
and that his accomplices had crept in through the
opening. She went through the anteroom to the
library. Here all was darkness and emptiness; but

the narrow little door leading into the passage was ajar. She could hear the cautious whispers of the men in the passage, and she had very little doubt they were already at work upon the iron door. She pushed the library door a little further open, and looked into the passage. There was a man on his knees before the iron door, working assiduously, upon that system of the progressive wedge, which is supposed to be infallible in such cases; another man was holding a pocket-lamp, which gave a vivid concentrated light just where it was wanted, and the third man, Tom Brook, was looking on, upon the watch, with eye and ear, for any interruption. A small black hand-bag on the ground held the instruments necessary for an artistic burglary; a couple of empty carpet-bags were ready to contain the spoil. Tom Brook stood two or three paces behind the two professional burglars. Elizabeth stole close up to him, and laid her hand lightly on his arm.

"Tom, I want to speak to you," she said, in a low voice.

He turned sharply round, clutched her wrist in his fierce grip, and held her as in a vice.

"What are you doing here?" he muttered savagely.

"Watching you. I have been watching you from the music-gallery for the last hour. I saw you at the supper, and knew you in spite of your red wig. If you will get away quietly with those men, without taking anything out of this house, I will not give the alarm; I will tell no one about you."

"You give the alarm!" said Mr. Brook. "I should like to see you do it! You, indeed! I'd soon stop your little pipe."

"I will do it, unless you take those men away this instant. This house shall not be robbed—this house, which has sheltered me—if I can prevent it!"

"You're a nice young woman to cheek your lawful husband like that," said Tom Brook, with his eye always looking beyond her towards the end of the dark passage, his keen ear always on the alert for any sound of approaching footsteps. "Come, Bess, don't be a fool. I didn't spoil your game; don't you spoil mine. You go to bed, and let us do our work quietly, without hurting anybody. If you try to make a row there'll be murder."

"You had better go before any one stirs," she said resolutely, fearless, although he had her in his grip. "There are plenty of men in the Castle. If the alarm is once given, you won't get off, you or your accomplices. I might have rung the alarm-bell, and had the whole house up five minutes ago; but I didn't want you to be caught. You had better get off quietly, now, while there's a chance."

"You had better hold your noise," said Tom Brook, taking a knife out of his pocket, and unclasping it with his teeth, his right hand still grasping Elizabeth's wrist.

In a moment he had swung her down on her knee, he had the blade at her throat, with intent to frighten and to silence her, perhaps, rather than to slay, although his looks were deadly enough as he scowled down at her.

She defied him even then, and, lifting up her voice, shrieked loud and shrill—a shriek that thrilled through the silent vaulted hall, and rang up to the roof, like the sound of a clarion.

Before that wild cry died into silence, the alarm-bell rang clamorously above the roof, calling help from far and wide, as it had rung two hundred and thirty years ago in the Civil Wars, and only once since then, on a summer night, in the reign of George III., when there had been an alarm of fire, beginning and ending in smoke. Tom Brook, not so hardened as the professional brotherhood, hesitated. He did not want to murder this creature, who had done all the harm it was in her power to do him, and who now crouched at his feet breathless, exhausted, looking up at him defyingly even in her helplessness. What could he gain by killing her? All chance of getting into the plate-room was

over now; the men had only to make their escape.
They huddled their tools together into the black
bag, made for the open window of the anteroom,
just as a figure carrying a candle in one hand and
a pistol in the other appeared at the end of the
passage. The men dashed into the library, the
shortest cut to the exit they wanted. But the man
who went through the library door last had caught
sight of that approaching figure. He clapped to
the door, and locked it, thus securing a safe retreat
for himself and his friend. Tom Brook, who was
an outsider, but who had put up the robbery, was
thus caught in a trap. He could not follow his
friends, but had to make good his own escape in
the teeth of the enemy.

He had that knife in his hand, that stout Shef-
field blade, which seemed made for murder. His
quick eye told him that the bell had as yet brought
only that one assailant. It was a question of moments. Half a minute more, and the scared half-
awakened household might be upon him. This
man must have been awake and dressed, for he
had come at the first sound of the bell.

Tom Brook flung off his wife, and made a rush
for the only outlet, the end of the passage which
led into the hall, through which he could double
back to the open window in the anteroom, and then

off across the snow as swift as a stag, to the cold covert of leafless woods.

But as he sprang forward the other man rushed upon him. It was Bruno Challoner.

Before Bruno could do anything—he had no intention of using the pistol, except in self-defence—Tom Brook lifted his knife and grappled with him. Elizabeth saw them close in what seemed a death-struggle: she sprang to her feet, and, as Bruno threw off his antagonist, who fell back a pace or two for a second spring, the girl flung herself between the two men, and the blow, intended for Bruno, fell, with all Tom Brook's savage strength, upon the breast of his wife.

She gave one low shuddering cry, and sank upon Bruno's arm. He clasped her to his breast, bathed in her life-blood, with his left arm, while with the right he took a steady aim at her murderer, and would have shot him dead, if his hand had not been arrested by Lord Ingleshaw, who came upon the group just in time to prevent this wild justice. The house-steward was with his master. Both had huddled on their clothes and rushed down to the hall at the sound of the alarm-bell, which had been rung by Mrs. Prince, who had been overtaken by sleep before the fire in her own cosy parlour, after the comfortable Christmas supper, while watching the little silver saucepan of mulled wine which she was preparing as a restorative for Elizabeth May. The wine had all boiled away when Mrs. Prince was awakened from that slumber by the awful sound of Elizabeth's shriek. She had rushed at once to the little stone vestibule, where the rope of the alarm-bell hung, fully possessed by the idea that the Castle was in flames. When she looked round her, and saw only moonlight and shadow, she began to think that wild long shriek must have been an incident in a dream.

Lord Ingleshaw and his steward secured Tom Brook, and wrenched the knife out of his hand before he could do any more mischief. He did not look as if he meant to renew the attack. Ghastly white, and with unspeakable horror in his countenance, he stared at his murdered wife, as her pallid face, with death dreadfully visible in every feature, lay on Bruno Challoner's breast, the glazing eyes looking up at him with infinite unconquerable love—love now made divine by the glory of a soul passing to the spirit-land.

"I saved you!" she murmured with her last breath, happier in that one moment of supernal bliss than some women have been in the lukewarm joys of a long lifetime,

Lucille's wedding was deferred from January to
April—the season of tender promise, of primroses
and violets, budding hedgerows, burgeoning trees,
the life and light that herald the coming of summer.
She and Bruno had both willed it so. They would
not be married while the odour of death was in the
house—while the earth that covered Elizabeth's
coffin in Ingleshaw churchyard had still the freshness of newly-dug mould—before even the flowers
could take root above that humble village grave, a
grave whose headstone bore only the name "Elizabeth," with the date of her death, and the words—
"Valued much and lamented much," below it.

She who was nothing to them, neither by kindred nor by equality of rank or fortune—who had
come and gone out of their lives like a dream, had
vanished like a tale that is told, leaving no token
behind her—had yet influenced the lives of both
too deeply to be easily forgotten, or to be thought
of lightly now she was gone.

In the chill winter gloaming, while the dead
girl was lying in the little room at the end of the
corridor, her narrow white bed strewn with Christmas roses, snowdrops, and white hyacinths, Bruno
Challoner made a full confession to his betrothed,
they two sitting alone by the fireside, in Lucille's
morning-room. He told her how weak he had been,

how strongly tempted, and how near he had been to falling. He testified to the loyalty of her who was gone. He bared his heart in all its strength, in all its weakness, to the woman who was to be his wife, and, by that perfect confidence, strengthened the bond between them as only truth can strengthen and sanctify such ties.

"O Bruno, I am so thankful to you for telling me this!" faltered Lucille, when he had said his last word. "Nothing less than this could have given me perfect peace—perfect confidence in you and your love. I knew that there was a time when you cared for her—yes, when your heart had been lured away from me by her strange beauty, by all her wayward unconscious graces and charms—and I knew that she loved you. I guessed her secret that night on board the yacht, and there was a time when I almost hated her. But God helped me somehow to bear that agony; and I prayed for patience; for I thought if I were patient your love would come back to me—you had loved me too long to forget me easily. It was a habit of your life to love me; and the old, old love, the love of all our happy years, could not so easily be trampled out of life. I thought of that big bay-tree in the garden, and how, after it had been cut down to the roots one severe winter, a new tree sprang up in its place, and grew and flourished with a wonderful growth, because the old roots were so strong and deep, the gardener said. And I thought that your love was too deeply rooted to be killed by one frost; and I waited and hoped; but I never felt sure I had not lost you till Christmas-eve, when you came back to me after our parting; and then I saw in your eyes, in your dear smile, that you were all my own again, my true and loyal lover, my true knight, without fear or blame. We will always think tenderly of her who is gone, dear, for she loved us both, and was true to us both. We will remember her, and be sorry for her sad fate all the days of our lives."

Bruno had told Lucille about the tie between Tom Brook and the dead girl. Mr. Brook was now awaiting the result of the adjourned inquest, in the lock-up at the market-town. His two accomplices had been caught in the park by the Ingleshaw gamekeepers, roused from their beds by the Castle bell, and ready to capture the first stranger encountered. The men had been caught red-handed, as it were—with the implements of their felonious trade about them—and they were in the lock-up at the market-town, awaiting the issue of an inquiry before the magistrates.

That inquiry resulted in the committal of the

two men for an attempted burglary, while Tom Brook was committed for manslaughter, of which crime he was duly convicted at the spring assizes, when his accomplices were sentenced to seven years' penal servitude, he, Tom, having turned Queen's evidence, and revealed the whole plan of the robbery. Tom, having thus made himself a useful instrument in furthering the ends of justice, got off lightly for so small a thing as a wife's life, and was allotted only a three years' seclusion from society and active usefulness.

The violets were in bloom on Elizabeth's grave when Lucille and Bruno were married one fair morning in late April. They left the churchyard gate in the carriage which was to take them to the station, from which they were to begin their honeymoon travels; and scarcely was the carriage out of sight when the inhabitants of Ingleshaw, rich and poor, laid their heads together to counterbalance this quiet wedding by a grand display of triumphal arches, flowers, flags, fireworks, and school-children, in honour of the young couple's home-coming.

THE END.

PRINTING OFFICE OF THE PUBLISHER.

www.ingramcontent.com/pod-product-compliance
Lightning Source LLC
Chambersburg PA
CBHW030645030726
47497CB00006B/1963